Timothy Daniel O'Sullivan

Dunboy

And other Poems

Timothy Daniel O'Sullivan

Dunboy
And other Poems

ISBN/EAN: 9783337206390

Printed in Europe, USA, Canada, Australia, Japan

Cover: Foto ©Andreas Hilbeck / pixelio.de

More available books at **www.hansebooks.com**

DUNBOY,

AND OTHER POEMS.

DUNBOY,

AND OTHER POEMS.

BY

TIMOTHY DANIEL O'SULLIVAN.

DUBLIN:

JOHN F. FOWLER,

3 CROW STREET.

MDCCCLXI.

J F FOWLER, PRINTER.
3 CROW STREET, 3 CROW STREET,
DUBLIN.

TO THE READER.

It may be well to inform the reader, in this place that the incidents in the poem of *Dunboy* are historical, not imaginary. The poem is written chiefly from the account of the siege given in the *Pacata Hibernia*, than which no fuller or more detailed account is extant. To found on the fortunes of Donal O'Sullivan and his family an interesting historical romance, would be a noble and a patriotic work—one which has been suggested in one of his speeches by the illustrious O'Connell—but the writer of the following poem has not attempted to do more than versify an existing authentic narrative, adding merely such minor details as may be supposed to have accompanied the graver events set down in history.

Dublin, November 16, 1860.

CONTENTS.

DUNBOY.

Tread where we may on Irish ground,
  From Antrim's coast to wild Cape Clear,
From East to West, no view is found
Without some ruin, rath, or mound
  To tell of times that were ;
Some lone round tower, yet strong and tall,
  Though swept by many a wasting age ;
Some wayside Cross, or abbey wall,
  With marks of man's unholy rage ;
Some graven slab, or giant stone,
  Notched with old signs and legends dim,
Some hallowed nook, with green o'ergrown,
  Or mouldering castle, bare and grim.
Initial letters, all and each,
  Of many a wild and curious story,
Mute tongues, that, silent, ever preach
  Of Ireland's past of grief and glory.

Oft at the crimson set of day
   I've gazed upon some war-worn pile,
And dreamed 'twas life-blood ebbed away
   Through those red chinks that gleamed the while.
Oft when the night came dark and cold,
   I've sat upon the weed-grown floor,
Where once the white-haired harper told
Of gallant deeds to clansmen bold;
At last, where battle-thunder rolled,
   And foemen slipped in gore.
The scene is changed—no shout, no cheer,
No din of combat meets the ear,
   No rafters ring to music now;
On the damp hearth the chill rain falls,
   Stout ash trees grow within the halls,
And in an angle of the walls
   The peasant stores his idle plough.

But most I loved a wreck that crowned
   A bright green bank, whose rocky base
The blue tide circled half way round
   As if 'twould clasp in fond embrace,
And sever from less honoured ground,
   The glorious soil, the hallowed place.
Yet few, upon that grassy heap,
   The marks to bid a stranger know
A castle's wood and stones lie deep,
And weapons rust, and heroes sleep,
   Its cloak of glistening green below.

Of one square tower the shattered butt
  Alone arrests the gazer's eye,
The ruins of a peasant's hut
  Above the earth might stand as high ;
The hollow where a trench had been
  Is rounded like a summer wave,
The ruined breastwork lifts the green
  No higher than a baby's grave—

Dunboy! Dunboy! the proud, the strong,
The Saxon's hate and trouble long,
All Ireland's hope, Momonia's boast,
The pride of Beara's iron coast—
These grass-grown heaps, this crumbling wall,
This low green ridge—can these be all
That war and time have left to tell
Where, long assailed, and foughten well,
Thy lofty turrets crashing fell ?

No more remains ; he seeks no more,
  Who knows the story of the past ;
He looks to find no stair or door,
No loop-holed frontage by the shore,
  With shade into the water cast ;
But o'er the wreck his reverent eyes
  Build up the picture from his brain,—
Walls, turrets, roofs, in thought arise,
  And Beara's flag flies out again.

A firm built pile, of simple shape,
    One plain square hall and slender tower,
Dunboy stood on the rocky cape,
    The central sign of Beara's power.
No threatening works its base enwound,
    No cunning fences flanked the way,
Its outworks were the hills around,
    Its ditch, a blue slip off the bay,
Stretching along for many a mile,
Shut in by one long mountain isle,
    Whose points approached the land so nigh,
That Beara's watchful men would strain
Across the strait a heavy chain
    When hostile ships would boldly try
To force an entrance from the main.
But calm and bright the lake-like sheet
    Beneath those rough hills ever smiled,
When fierce waves on the sea coast beat,
    When winds were howling high and wild,
And madly tossed the sea-ward fleet,
Each vessel in that safe retreat
    Rocked like the cradle of a child.
Brown sailors, weary of the sea
    Of summer calm and winter gale,
Would often say 'twas sweet to be
    The chief of that secluded vale,
The owner of that castle tall,
    The lord of harbour, plain, and hill,
With clansmen ready at a call
    To work their master's lightest will.

But not a ship upon the sea
   Nor town nor tower upon the shore
Obeyed a chief more brave than he
   Whose honoured flag that castle bore,—
O'Sullivan, the Prince of Beare
   And Bantry of the spacious bay—
A name his foemen heard with fear,
   But loved by all who owned his sway;
One of the proud Eugenian line
   Of Heber's blood, from Eoghan sprung,
Shoots of the grand old Spanish vine[1]
   By scholars traced and poets sung.

Brave Donal! foes and traitors knew
His spirit high, and feared it too;
While young or old, the poorest man,
Matron or maid, amongst his clan,
Whose cause was good, whose claim was just,
In his true heart might safely trust,
And ask from his superior might
Support and succour for the right.
Strong-boned, but spare of flesh was he,
As slight trees grow beside the sea,
Yet tall and straight; his stately form
Seemed well inured to sun and storm.
His face was thin, his light brown hair
Half hid a forehead smooth and fair;
Fast came his thoughts whene'er he spoke,
From his blue eyes quick flashes broke;

But while he mused, or walked alone,
His features took another tone,
And slow of step he moved along,
Like one inwrapt in love or song.
Yet ever in that manly breast
The passion ruling all the rest,
The source to which his thoughts returned,
The central fire that in him burned,
By life's own forces fed and fanned,
Was pure love of his native land.
Fit chieftain he his clan to sway
From that tall castle by the bay,
Whose firm and well embattled front
Seemed built to bear war's fiercest brunt,
Yet whose broad halls were warm and bright
With music, laughter, love, and light,
Whose strong walls held a quiet nook
Where stood the Cross and holy Book,
Where bended knees and reverent feet
    By night and day the flooring trod,
Whence many a prayer, in accents sweet
    Went through the turrets up to God.

Stern Donal! many a care and pain
Tried that great soul, that brilliant brain:
Rude shocks of war, and subtler art,
Broke vainly on that gallant heart,
    And only proved, when all was done,
A patriot pure and true till death

A hero to his latest breath
  Was Beara's Prince, O'Sullivan.

———

A scene of peace was Beara's vale
For months, and years, while through "the Pale",
Along our northern mountain chains,
·And o'er our fertile midland plains,
The war for faith and freedom, waged
By gallant Hugh O'Neill, had raged.
River and fort and pass had seen
The routed troops of England's queen
Bleed, gasp, and drown, or fly the land
  'Till death or distance hid from view
The Banner of the Blood-Red Hand,
  And hushed the shout "Lamh Dearg Abu!"
And many a fierce and bloody raid
The well-armed Saxon troops had made;
Oft had they swept, in barbarous ire,
O'er towns and fields with sword and fire,
Left where they passed but trampled lawns,
And blackened fields, and empty bawns.
The flames of village roof-trees showed
  The way their ruthless forces went;
Dismantled churches marked their road
  With many a mournful monument.

Disease, and Irish swords, cut down
　　Their ranks, but fresh invaders came;
Their cruel queen would lose her crown,
　　Or win at last the bloody game.
Yet dared the bold O'Neill to cope
　　With all her world-known wealth and might;
In Irish arms he placed his hope,
With succour from the holy Pope,
　　And Spain's good King, to aid the right.
Gladly the looked-for help was given—
　　The Royal Pontiff blest the cause,
And prayed the choicest grace of Heaven
On those brave men to battle driven
　　For Christ's pure faith and Erin's laws.
Deep chests of gold King Philip sent
With notice of his fixed intent
To aid the strife as 'twere his own,
Not with his steel or gold alone—
A portion of his army brave,
　　Full well equipped and nobly led,
Would soon be speeding o'er the wave
　　To join the native force, he said,
And sweep the isle, from coast to coast
Free of the savage Saxon host.

'Twas blessèd news—a tale of joy,
It filled the land, it reached Dunboy;
'Twas told by many a peasant's hearth
　　While young and old were circled round,

And many a war-like wish had birth,
 And many a heart would gladly bound,
As great King Philip's praise was rung
In rich rolls of the Irish tongue.
Upon the hills 'twas argued o'er
 When clansmen, friends, or neighbours met,
'Twas long discussed on sea and shore,
 By fishers tending boat and net.
The very crones, low bent and old,
 Talked bravely of the mighty King,
In flowing periods proudly told
His men, his ships, his store of gold,
 The force the promised fleet would bring,
To win again the Irish lands
From out the robber Saxons' hands,
And chase from off the Irish sod
Those murderers of the saints of God.

So spoke his people one and all,
So swelled the voice of hut and hall,
When pacing slow, one summer day,
 Before his castle, by the tide
The Prince of Beara paused to say
 To gallant clansmen at his side—
" Our country calls! why dream we here ?
 Her cries have pierced beyond the main
Why linger midst the hills of Beare
 While aids arrive from distant Spain,

When he who sits where Peter sate,
    Holding within his saintly hands,
The keys of Heaven's eternal gate,
    Has blest our patriot Irish bands,
And cheered with like rewards, their work,
    Who fight the Saxon and the Turk?[2]
Up! up! my men, but yestere'en
    My fastest craft brought in the tale—
The Spaniard's stately ships were seen
    Within the harbour of Kinsale;
From their huge sides unto the shore
    Brave soldiers by the hundred went,
And to each fort a goodly store
    Of all the needs of war was sent.
Come let us call from hill and coast
    All Beare and Bantry's fighting men,
And haste to join that gallant host,
    Who raise our country's hopes again!
What though in London's gloomy tower
    Desmond and brave MacCarthy pine,[3]
And Munster's boldest chieftains cower,
Before Carew's and Thomond's power,
    The grander cause is yours and mine!
No boon, no gift we own to day
    From the fierce Queen of England's hands:
We spurn her peace, we cast away
    Her patent for our fathers' lands,[4]
And read our rights, not from her scrolls,
But on our swords and in our souls!

Come let us forth : whoe'er may fail
    Whoe'er may falter or delay,
We join the camp before Kinsale—
    What do my trusty clansmen say ?"

They answered loud, the words he spoke
Glad echoes in their hearts awoke ;
They loved to meet their country's foes
    On battle fields, with axe and lance,
As maidens, blooming like the rose,
    Loved the sweet song and merry dance.
A foul and loathsome thing, they said,
    The traitor's heart must ever be,
The wretch whose life it feeds, must
    dread
    To look within himself and see :
And little purer is his heart
    Who hears his country's battle cry—
    Who sees her red strife raging nigh—
Yet cowers and shrinks and stands apart,
    Irresolute, afraid to die ;
Or who with furtive eye looks on
    And marks the fortunes of the fight,
Prepared, when all is lost and won,
    To join the victor, wrong or right—
Ready to worship fraud and guilt ;
    Or should they fail, as quick to claim
A glory in the bright blood spilt
    In truth's good cause, in freedom's name.

The chieftain's face with pleasure glowed
As towards his castle gate he strode,
But darkened with a shade of thought
   As, drawing near the loop-holed walls,
Sweet tones the charmèd breezes brought
   In full soft swells and gentle falls.
He knew her voice—his Eileen fair!
   He felt its harp-like ripples run,
He knew the wild, yet plaintive air
   That hushed to sleep his darling son.
"Heaven guard", he said, "my lights of life,
My children dear, my gentle wife!
God save young Donal! may he be
A Prince in Erin glad and free,
A chief of fame on land and sea!
Young Donal, were I asked to-day,
To look my whole life through, and say,
Since first a human utterance stirred
   My heart with news of joy or woe,
What was the happiest tale I heard,
   I'd own 'twas said five years ago
In that short speech, that simple one,
That told me of your birth, my son.
God keep us! times of change are these—
A Prince one day, the next day sees
A houseless wanderer, robbed and banned,
With strangers fattening on his land;
For only those who bend and bow
To foreign churls are nobles now—

But He who reads my spirit, knows
   I'd rather see my name and race
Stamped out by Ireland's brutal foes
   Than flourish through such dire disgrace".

So mused the Prince as soft he stept
Where Eileen sung and Donal slept.
Their greetings o'er, the sunny smile
Evanished from his face awhile,
And once again the painful thought
Its change upon his features wrought;
But soon it passed—his dark eye burned
With love's pure light, as full he turned
   To her whose heart, however deep
Its gushing love, for ever gave
   Such counsel as a Prince might keep,
And still be bravest of the brave:
And thus he said—

        "My Eileen dear,
I know I scarcely need to say
   That Donal's heart is ever here,
Let Honour call him where she may,—
   With you, with this dear boy, and those
Sweet babes whose years are fewer still,
   But well my gentle Eileen knows
That Donal's duty shapes his will.
To-day——"
        He paused, but Eileen said—

"My Donal, I have heard the tale,
And guessed your thoughts; but never dread
My well-tried heart even now will fail.
King Philip's aids have come at length
Our country and our faith to free,
And you would go, with Beara's strength
To join the strife.—Ah, woe is me!
What can I do but sigh and pray
Above my babes—a sad employ—
And sorrowing gaze each weary day
Across the hills from lone Dunboy!"

Around her trembling form he threw,
With light touch like a tendril's clasp,
Those great strong arms his foemen knew
So forceful in their hostile grasp;
And said in murmurs soft and low—
"God bless and guard you well, mo stor:
Those troubled days that come and go
But make me love you more and more;
As fruit is ripened on the tree,
And flowers are touched with charming
bloom,
Not by one heaven of brilliancy,
But skies of changing light and gloom.
Not in Dunboy, my Eileen dear,
My babes shall sleep and you shall pray,
Lest war and fire should gather here
While Beara's troops are far away.

Our brave old castle for a time
  A Spanish force shall have and hold,
Sure gunners, tried in many a clime,
  And chosen swordsmen, quick and bold.
From these no prowling English foes
  Shall take our home beside the sea,
No traitorous Irish, worse than those,
  The masters of our land shall be ;
But you shall stay, my cherished wife,
  In wild, but warm Glengariffe, where
No sights or sounds of deadly strife
  Shall fright your eye or shock your ear.
The wind through bright arbutus trees
  And low oak woods, the blackbird's song,
Sweet river music mixt with these
  Shall softly speed your days along ;
And oh, let dreams as calmly sweet
  And hopes as bright, your comfort be,
Till once again I come to meet
  My own dear wife, mo stor, machree!"

Through all the castle quickly fled
The warlike words the Prince had said ;
The women whispered, half alarmed,
  With looks and signs that boded ill ;
The hardy kerns smiling armed
  To try was all in order still ;
Shook their long spears with handles tough,
  Stretched their strong arms and o'er them drew

Their jackets made of hempen stuff
  With small steel rings worked on and through;
Felt their good skeans along the edge,
  And laughing pulled their beards and glibs,
And told when last each slender wedge
  Went in between a foeman's ribs!
The stern old bard looked proudly round
  And eyed the group, as if to say,
To him they owed that victory crowned
  Their efforts on each battle day!
Then to his honoured seat he strode,
  Placed his loved harp between his knees,
Sweet preludes from his fingers flowed,
  And then he sung such words as these,
Unto an air that rippled first,
  Then swelled and shook his strings of gold,
Then loud as summer thunder burst,
  And through the castle echoing rolled :—

I.

Who will hold back when O'Sullivan, loudly,
  Calls on his people to haste to his aid?
Who will not rush to him, gladly and proudly,
  Fire in his heart and an edge on his blade?
      Kindred! clansmen!
      Seamen and landsmen!
Young men and old men, a-far and a-near!
      Together! together!
      In calm or wild weather,
When called by the shout of O'Sullivan Beare!

II.

Never a coward, a cringer or quailer,
  Was chieftan of Beara of late or of yore;
Ever a hero, a soldier and sailor,
  Mighty at sea and resistless on shore!
    Landsmen! seamen!
    Fearless and free men!
Namesakes and kinsmen a-far and a-near!
    Together! together!
    From sea-foam and heather
Come on to the call of O'Sullivan Beare!

III.

Come with a rush when O'Sullivan needs you,
  Worthy your cheerful devotion is he!
Gaily dash on where O'Sullivan leads you,
  Fearing not, caring not, where it may be!
    Tall men! small men!
    Stout men and all men,
Horsemen and boatmen a-far and a-near!
    Together! together!
    In calm or wild weather
When called by the shout of O'Sullivan Beare!

Where was the heart that would not spring
  To notes like these, the listeners said,
Such quickening words and tones should bring
  A clansman from his dying bed.

'Twas well to have, before the fray
While redly loomed the battle day
   Such music surging through the brain:
It nerved the hand that held the spear,
It filled the veins with fire, to hear
   So wild, so bold a strain!

The evening sped, the thin gray night
Passed quickly on ; but ere the light
Of morning touched the eastern bound
Of Beare or Bantry's rugged ground,
The news had spread, the Prince's call
Had reached his warriors one and all.
They came from near and far away,
   From headlands bold, and sheltered creeks,
The bearded fishers of the bay
   With calm gray eyes and hollow cheeks,
With hands like iron, hard and brown,
   And hearts that never knew despair,
When wild and black the storm came down,
   And only Heaven could see and hear
   Their wave-tossed craft, their heartfelt pray'r.
The merrier children of the hills,
   With faces red as evening skies,
With firmer steps, with fiercer wills,
   With quicker passions in their eyes.
Some who had borne the brunt before
   Of deadly battle, but who felt
Their hands could deal good blows once more,
   If not such blows as once they dealt ;

And glowing youths, who never yet
A foe in mortal combat met,
But whose hearts' hope was now to be
The foremost rank of all,—to see
And smite the churls who dared be found
As Ireland's foes on Irish ground.
All day they came, and days passed by
    And saw them still assembling there,
They paused to shape, to fit and try
    Their dress and weapons : sword and spear
They stuck into the earth upright
    And blest with many a form and pray'r.[5]
They bade them flash like blinding light,
And break not, bend not, through the fight,
Nor ever glance or turn aside,
    But striking keen, whate'er the part,
Find out the mortal vein, and glide
    Right onward towards the foeman's heart !

At length arrived the marching day,
    And all was ready—every man
    His duty knew, and Donal's plan,
And all cried out to lead the way !
The Prince strode forward to a mound,
    And, looking back, beheld with joy
The hundreds of his clan and race
With patriot fire in every face
Who stood like living ramparts round
    The gray walls of Dunboy !

He gave the word to march!—A shout
   Of stormy gladness upward rushed,
The morning sun shone redly out,
   And all the landscape purple flushed!
The bristling mass moved gaily on,
And ere one bright'ning hour was gone,
   The latest ranks were lost to sight;
But twice or thrice—so rough the ground—
The force was seen as slow it wound
Some mountain's base or headland round,
   Or climbed some sudden height.
Then silence brooded over Beare
And by Dunboy; the sharpest ear
In passing by could only hear
   The mimic waves, the whispering breeze,
Or drawing near the castle walls,
The warders' tread through empty halls,
   And clanking of their keys.

———

Not many days had fleeted by
   Since Donal left his mountain home,
When from Beare island's summit high,
The anxious watchers could descry
A foreign war-ship drawing nigh,
   And pitching through the foam.

She crossed the bay, she swept around
The island's western point, and found
   The harbour's safest way,
And those who saw her passage, knew
Berehaven pilots steered her to
   The mooring where she lay.
Brass guns peeped through her rounded side,
   Her stern was carved, and blazed with gold,
Bright saints looked mildly on the tide,
   And wingéd angels stooped to hold
The painted ribbon, opening wide,
   Whereon her name was grandly scrolled.
Her prow was curled and gilded too,
   And from her topmasts slim and high
The Spanish colours proudly flew,
   A welcome sign to every eye.

Soon from her deck the sailors lowered
Their painted pinnace, many-oared,
Upon her planks the light crew sprung,
Rich cloaks upon her seats were flung,
Then gallant chiefs whose dress was bright
With rich rewards for many a fight,
Stepped in, and soon were rowed to land
   Beneath Dunboy, where all leaped out,
Sunk their sharp anchor in the strand,
   Then sauntered on and gazed about;
Marked how the castle looked and bore
On wood and mound and winding shore,

What parts were strong, what walls were weak,
Which point assailants first would seek,
Where were the nooks and rooms, the ward
Should strive the best to arm and guard.
The soldiers sought the castle then,
   The sailors hastened to their boat,
Rowed to their ship, and back again
With such a load of arms and men
   The pinnace scarce could float.
Berehaven craft, strong built and wide,
Came clustering round the vessel's side,
And loaded deep with precious freights
Of larger bulks and greater weights;
Huge chests of powder, long black guns,
Large balls in heaps of many tons,
Casks of the flesh of Spanish kine,
And sacks of corn and butts of wine.
The castle vaults soon held the stores,
They touched the roofs and jammed the doors:
The guns were mounted on the walls,
The merry soldiers filled the halls,
And through thin slits and windows strong
Came many a snatch of foreign song.
The ship's appointed work was done,
   She spread her white wings to the wind,
From her high deck a farewell gun
   Sung out to those she left behind.
Around the castle soon a crowd
   Of gallant sons of Spain appeared,

They waved their hats and shouted loud,
While back from yard and stay and shroud
   The hardy seamen cheered!
First for the holy Faith, and then,
   The best of Kings, the King of Spain,
Then good old Ireland and the men
   He sent them to sustain!
The good ship glided fast away
   Before a freshening northern gale,
Again she crossed the broad blue bay
   And headed for Kinsale.

Some dreary winter weeks had past,
The longest night its shade had cast
   O'er Ireland far and near—
When darker than that darkest night,
A rumour of the distant fight
Came like a wind whose breath was blight,
   Across the hills of Beare.
An anxious crowd of young and old
   Thronged wildly round each panting scout,
Ah, evil news is quickly told
   And thus they gasped it out :—

"Donal is hastening back again
 With shattered ranks from lost Kinsale!
O'Donnell steers away for Spain,
 And northward speeds O'Neill!
O fatal night! O woful day!
The Irish troops like sand gave way,
And Ireland's cause is lost for aye!"

"Donal is hastening back to Beare",
 New comers cried, "from curst Kinsale!
Plague on the sleepy Spaniards there,
Who would not watch, and did not hear
That midnight battle raging near,
 And rising o'er the gale!
All, all went wrong; some wretched man
Forewarned the foe, betrayed the plan.
O'Donnell madly led the van,
 But led them on to fail?
A panic seized the Irish host,
They broke, they fled, the day was lost—
First of the ranks still firm and true,
Were Donal's, Beara's, gallant few,[6]
 But what could they avail!
O fatal night! O woful day!
'Twas long foretold, the wise men say,[7]
'Twas toil and blood thrown all away!"

But later comers brought the news,
With sharper lines and darker hues,

And added points of woe—
"O day", they cried, "of shame and grief!
Don Juan—curse the coward chief!—
Whom Philip sent to our relief,
  Has truckled to the foe,
Has hauled the Spanish colours down,
And rendered, not alone the town
He proudly promised to maintain
'For Christ and for the King of Spain',
But every rood of land we gave
His dainty troops to guard and save;
Finin O'Driscoll's castles strong
Of Donneshed and Dun-na-long,
Donogh O'Driscoll's castle too,
By Castlehaven's waters blue;
All these the crafty wretch, Carew,
  Will hasten to destroy—
And then, the craven, last and worst,
Agreed to yield our foes accurst
  Our castle! our Dunboy!
O fatal night! O woful day!
Our castle tricked and signed away!
Our good cause lost, and lost for aye!"

What grief, of all the griefs of men,
  Can rend the heart, can crush the brain,
Like his—the patriot soldier—when
  His country's fight is fought in vain;

When dazzling hopes in gloom are quenched;
　　When freedom, right, and old renown
On native fields, with good blood drenched,
　　Beneath the invader's feet go down;
When crime in gay success can bask,
　　When virtue's meeds are woe and blight,
And tortured hearts will almost ask,
　　Lives there a God of truth and right?
What nobler soul to man is given
　　Than his who holds, through storm and ill,
A changeless trust in righteous Heaven,
　　A patriot love that nought can chill?
Such grief and love, so firm a faith,
　　Was Donal's when he took his way
Back from Kinsale's red fields of death,
　　And sought his home by Bantry Bay;
Not shelter 'midst those hills to seek,
　　Till past the storm of war had blown,
And then in pleadings low and meek
　　Ask mercy of the English throne;
But on the rugged heights of Beare
　　In arms for freedom yet to stand,
And hold, though crushed the strife elsewhere.
One fortress safe for freedom there,
　　One flag erect in all the land!

Again O'Sullivan drew nigh
　　The home he left in hope and pride;
Soon as its broad flag met his eye,
　　He called his trustiest chiefs aside—

Brave Tyrrell, leader of a band
    Who ever sought war's wildest work,
Donal Mac Carthy, strong of hand,
    With wise and valiant William Burke;
The Lord of Lixnaw and his men,
    Who from the glades of Kerry came,
O'Connor, and the Knight of Glyn,
    With other chiefs of lesser name;
Upon the rough hill's side they sate,
    And talk'd their country's rise or fall,
Till summing up their calm debate,
    Prince Donal spoke the minds of all :—

"We must win back Dunboy from those
Who mean to yield it to our foes,
By force or wile, by night surprise,
Or storm beneath the noon-day skies.
A chosen force we then must send
Our mountain passes to defend,
Glengariffe first and best of all,
For there a band, though weak and small,
May check an army on its way,
And hold ten times their force at bay.
But lest our safeguards all should fail,
And Saxon might awhile prevail,
Lest troops should force Glengariffe through
And Beara see the curséd crew,
And, though 'tis hard to even suppose
Dunboy a home for Ireland's foes,

Yet, lest even that befal, 'tis meet
We now mark out a last retreat.

The Dursy island rises high
　　And bluff from out the angry tide;
Fierce currents sweep for ever by,
A stranger force will scarcely try
　　To land on either side;
We'll send a few brave men to keep
The forts upon its summit steep;
Of arms and food a plenteous store,
　　Drawn from Dunboy, we'll send before:
Then should the worst befal us here,
We'll take our stand unyielding there".

On hastened Donal to demand
The trust he gave, his house and land;
But peaceful summons, threats or calls,
Brought not the Spaniards from his halls;
To each command the men replied
　　They knew the terms their chief had made
With Lord Carew, and would abide
　　By every word he signed and said.
Thus bearded at his very gate,
　　Donal his angry troops withdrew,
But had not long to watch and wait,
When fell a night as dark as fate,
　　And wild the west wind blew;
He brought his men with noiseless pace
Before the castle's eastern face,

Huge stones they picked and pulled away,
And towards the dawning of the day
    They burst their passage through!
Up screaming leaped the startled guard,
Down rushed and tumbled all the ward—
Bright swords gleamed out and muskets snapped,
Hard steel on steel opposing slapped,
    But Donal rushed to view.
My men, he cried, put up your swords!
You Spaniards too, obey my words!
No enemies or traitors we,
Your king shall answer if we be,
    And speak for what we do—
We stand for Spain and Ireland still,
And only cross Don Juan's will,
    The tool of vile Carew!
Behold my three best men are laid
In gasps of death from ball or blade,
Upon the bloody floor, and yet
I will not have my soldiers wet
    A single spear-point in your veins—
But, raise another hostile hand,
By Heaven! my men, who waiting stand
Without the walls, shall hack and slay
Till of your numbers here to-day
    No living man remains!"

Good Father Archer, often tried
In scenes as wild, stepped forth and cried :—

"Lay down your arms, ye men of Spain!
Brave troops in hundreds wait outside,
   And further strife is vain!
Know, too, your good and faithful king
   Will not approve Don Juan's course;
Soon other ships on rapid wing
Another captain here shall bring,
   To lead another force;
Lay down your arms; who strikes again
Is foe to Ireland, Rome, and Spain!

They flung their weapons on the floor:
   Then Donal said: "A pinnace fleet
Even now is waiting by the shore;
Let those who wish to aid no more
   Our Irish cause, but long to meet
Their fickle chieftain, step on board.
I pledge upon my trusty sword,
   A promise never known to fail,
My men shall bear them safely on,
And ere another day be gone
   Shall land them at Kinsale!

They paused a moment to decide,
Then onward marched towards the tide,
Save one small group of gunners, who
Would still remain to Donal true.
The boat was manned, her sails were spread,
Like a white sea-bird on she fled.

The Prince looked on till from his sight
She swept behind Beare island's height,
Then lightly smiled, as if to say,
One danger now had past away.

O'Sullivan, if craven fear
    Could reach your heart, 'twas now the time
To plead unto the Saxon's ear
    And call your patriot strife a crime;
For now is Munster swept to bring
    Together all that murderous band
Who almost blot the green of spring
    In blood and ashes from the land,
To crowd in one resistless mass
    The victor troops of many a field,
And trample down like sun-dried grass
    The clans that yet refused to yield.
Brave Donal, what shall save you when
    An army wraps your forces round—
All Ireland knows your valiant men
Would face their foemen one to ten
    And clear the battle ground;
But for each arm that wields to day
    A blade for Erin and for you,
A hundred in the tyrant's pay
    Are stretched to conquer and subdue;

And not alone the sword is bared
   And cannon crammed to reach your heart,—
No plot is spurned, no bribe is spared,
   No dark device of traitor art.*
But you have matched their might ere now
   And foiled their wiles; this new demand
On brain and heart but lights your brow
   And adds new vigour to your hand.
Not even a shudder shakes your frame,
   Though boding thought at times must show
Your princedom swept with sword and flame,
   Your clan o'erborne, your castle low;
Though o'er your kindly heart must fly
   Dark glooms of care for kith and kin,
Yet those who meet that calm blue eye
   See only fixed resolve within.
So may the brave man meet the strife,
   So calm the hero's soul may be,
When home and freedom, lands and life,
   Are staked for God and Liberty.

'Twas summer morn, the eastern skies
Were rich in gold and crimson dyes.
The sunshine, like a glorious rain,
Streamed from the east and steeped the plain;

But Beara's circling mountains kept
The bright flood from the vale that slept
Beneath their feet, until the sun
Raised high the tide, and streams would
    run
From clefts and hollows in the hills
Down to the vale like golden rills,
Each moment finding leaks anew,
That dazzling jets came shining through,
Till meeting, mingling, spreading wide,
The flood swept all the mountain side,
And Beara, like a golden cup,
With glorious light was brimming up!

That brilliant gush of morning light
Showed Donal's men a hated sight.
Close by the isle those dull black dots
    The last night's clouds too well concealed,
Stood plainly forth, the direst blots
    That e'er the noonday sun revealed.
A glance sufficed—a hundred lips
Cried out: "The ships—the English ships!"
Fast runners over hill and dale
Bore on the brief but startling tale.
"Ho! men", they said, "the strife is nigh!
The English ships at anchor lie
Within our harbour: hasten all
Now with your Prince to stand or fall!"

Soon on Beare isle the Saxons swarmed,
Close by the shore their camp they formed.
No petty force for trivial fray,
No fraction of an army they,—
Four thousand soldiers, trained and tried,
They came to Beara, well supplied
With arms and stores, commanded too
By skilful chiefs and captains, who
Had fought, and wrecked, and gathered spoil
From Galway down to Carrigfoyle.
Days flitted by on rapid wing,
   While Lords Carew and Thomond planned
Their ways and means to safely bring
   Nigh to Dunboy their troops to land.
A smaller island smiling lay
   So close beside the wished-for shore,
An army there might choose the day,
   The hour, to take their passage o'er;
There would they move their force, and then
   Their finest wit and skill employ,
To baffle and deceive the men
   Who watched and guarded round Dunboy,
Then on a sudden push across
   To some defenceless point, and there
Leap out and gain with little loss
   A footing on the soil of Beare.

But first Carew was fain to try
   A plan that served him oft before.

Some proffered bribe, he said, might buy
   A warder from the castle door,
That marksman from the castle wall
   Whose aim and gun were Beara's boast,
Some guard or scout, or best of all,
   The captain Donal trusted most.
He whispered Thomond what to do:
   He bade him threaten, bribe, cajole,
Sound him and spy him through and through,
   And strive to shake the rebel's soul,
Thus from his fears, his greed or guile,
   ' With half the threatened cost obtain
The end they'd marched so many a mile
   And toiled so long to gain.

It was agreed, and Thomond penned
   An offer to the Prince of Beare.
It said, " Your trustiest chieftain send
   To hold an hour of parley here ;
The spot where he and I shall stand
   The castle and the camp shall see ;
Some distance off on either hand
   A force shall wait for him and me ;
But, howsoe'er we may decide,
   For war or peace, our parley o'er,
Unharmed your man shall cross the tide
   And reach Dunboy once more".

So be it, Donal said, and soon
   Upon a well selected space,

Beneath the glowing sky of June,
   The chosen chiefs stood face to face.
One was a man of middle size,
   His port was firm, his glance was keen ;
But what the wrinkles near his eyes
   And lines around his mouth might mean,
The gazer failed awhile to know,
   Till at some turn, some word he spake,
The guile that filled his heart would show,
   His lips would hiss, his eyes would take
The serpent's cold and deadly glare,
   And every glint and glisten told
He might be foiled, but would not spare
   The victim once within his fold.
Such was the Earl of Thomond, who
Sprung from the line of great Born,
Yet, shameless, plied a traitor's sword
To aid a viler foreign horde
Than that whose power the monarch broke
And bowed beneath the Irish yoke.

The other was a larger form,
   A finer mould, with ease and grace
In his strong limbs ; much sun and storm
   Had deeply browned his manly face ;
Yet boyhood's smile would curve his lips
   And light his eyes, till thought or care
Would sudden come, and half eclipse
   Or dim the cheerful glories there.

Then stooped his eyebrows till they met
   Above the orbs they nearly hid,
And looked one level line of jet
   Beneath the stately pyramid
Of his great forehead. But again
   The clouds passed off; his heart would hurl
Its grief aside, or hide its pain,
   The long black line would break and curl
Again above his calm brown eyes,
   And face and form alike would show
He was a warrior, bold, but wise,
   A faithful friend, a gallant foe:
So stood the Prince's chosen man,
His best loved chief, Mac Geohagan.

First Thomond spoke. "Well pleased am I",
   He said, "to meet you, chieftain, here.
Behold, a mighty force is nigh,
And yet we pause and calmly try
   To save the haughty Prince of Beare.
Tell him we offer lands and life,
   Perhaps a title from the queen,
If he but cease this foolish strife,
   Adopt her creed, nor longer lean
For succour on the King of Spain,
Or Rome's proud priest, whose aid is vain".

Calmly replied Mac Geohagan:
   "Methinks, sir earl, his house and lands

3

He holds with all his gallant clan.
　　His life? 'tis in his Maker's hands!
A title?　Well, he boasts of two—
　　The Prince of Beare is surely one,
The other—not a strange or new,
But old and famous, good and true,
No monarch's gift; its glory grew
From noble deeds: All Ireland through
　　Who knows not The O'Sullivan?
Proud titles flow from England's throne:
My chief is happy with his own".

"It pales, it fades, even while you speak",
　　The earl replied.　"You sure must know,
That month by month, aye, week by week,
　　Such titles disappear, like snow
　　From trampled highways; where we go
Such tenures fail, are cloven through
　　By keen-edged swords, are reft and burned
Where'er our banners flout the blue,
　　Where'er our cannons' mouths are turned.
I too could summon for the fight
　　A force like yours: I too could send
Brave clans to break on England's might,
　　But whose the profit in the end?
Instead, I save my home, my land,
　　My wealth, my title, from the whirl
That gulps you down, and here I stand
No hapless outlaw, watched and banned,
　　But a high captain and an earl!

So may your master also be.
Go bid him from Carew and me
Surrender——"
        "No", the chief replied :
  If this be all, our task is done ;
Let further speech from either side
  Be spoken out from gun to gun.
The Prince of Beare rejects your bribes,
  Defies your queen, contemns her creed,
Heeds not your threats, flings back your gibes,
  And dares you now from word to deed !"

"Stay !" said the earl, "one moment stay :
  I now would speak a word with *you.*
Say will you waste your life away
  Amongst this doomed and desperate crew ? —
A brave young chieftain, formed to grace
  Gay scenes, and there the gayest shine—
Why hide within this lonely place,
  Between those mountains and the brine ?
Say will you join even now with us,
  And win the court's, the Queen's applause,
Or nameless die, maintaining thus
  A failing creed, a ruined cause ?"

Mac Geohagan moved back a pace,
  His broad chest heaved, his head rose higher,
Quick shadows flitted o'er his face,
  His eye balls gleamed like yellow fire :

But soon the rising fury died
    Within his heart; a sad half smile
Played round his lips as he replied:
    "I did forget a little while
The words, sir earl, were said by you:
    They hissed indeed upon my ear;
But when I ventured here, I knew
    The words I might expect to hear;
I therefore will not now complain
    Of honour wronged, but only say,
You try your subtle art in vain
    To wile my poor support away.
I know the peril; I have lost
    Ancestral lands and castles fair;[9]
I've paid down all the strife can cost
    Except my life, and that I dare
From day to day for Ireland's sake;
    I choose again the patriot's part,
And freely bid my country take
    The last red life-drop from my heart".

"We part", said Thomond, "soon to meet
Amid the battle's dust and heat,
Or in the captured castle, where
Your after thoughts we yet may hear".

"The castle? No", the chief returned,
While like twin stars his dark eyes burned—
"The castle? Never. Mark me well,
For time shall prove the truth I tell—

No English troops shall ever find
A shelter from the rain or wind,—
No English preacher ever raise
A canting hymn in England's praise,—
No English council ever prate
The weal or woe of England's State,
Nor Irish slave one hour enjoy,
Beneath the roof of proud Dunboy".

Unto his boat the chieftain strode;
The earl retraced his mountain road,
And to his anxious master told
How spoke the rebel, proud and bold.
" What! slighted thus", Carew out cried,
" My threats contemned, my force defied!
Thinks he his small half-armed pack
Shall chase my valiant regiments back?
His clan forsooth! some dozen score
Of paltry rogues. Good earl, no more.
Call in the boats, ship all the men,
Cross o'er to Deenish isle, and then
At dawning of some cloudy day,
Quick to the main-land make your way.
Soon from that time 'twill plain be seen
Who rules—the rebel, or the Queen".

To Deenish isle the transports bore
The reg'ments and their warlike store.
From thence the mainland's crookéd coast
Was distant half a mile at most

At points from whence the castle lay
Three miles of rugged ground away.
Again the boats moved from the isle,
Disguised their plan a little while,
Then steered to the appointed strand,
And safely bore their freights to land.

The clansmen hurried to oppose
The wily movement of their foes;
But ere they swept one half way round,
The troops were firm on Beara's ground.
Still on they came; drawn nigh at length
Amazed they saw the Saxon's strength,
The mighty mass of veteran troops
In ordered lines and busy groups,
The huge guns dotted o'er the green,
The heaps of smaller arms between,
The posts and works of wicker made
While on the larger isle they stayed,
And all that showed a force prepared
For all an army ever dared.
Dark looked the fortunes of the few
Who stood by Donal firm and true,
And witnessed in that gloomy hour
That dread array of England's power.
"Yet", shouted Tyrrell, "though we see
Those odds are fearful, shall it be
That those vile churls, this crew accurst,
Shall pass this night, and this their first,

On Beara's soil, and never feel
One vengeful point of Irish steel?
No, comrades no, ere set of sun,
Their yellow Saxon blood shall run
On the polluted soil, to show
Dunboy's first welcome to her foe!"

On rushed the Irish with a shout
　　That rang through all the hills around:
The English wheeled their ranks about
　　And formed upon the rising ground.
Loud burst war's tumult on the gale,
　　The cannons' sullen thunder rose,
The muskets launched their leaden hai
　　Red lightnings leapt amidst the foes,
Bright swords and polished daggers shone,
　　Sharp skeans gleamed out and hid again,
And crash and curse, and stab and groan,
　　Mixed in one roar of rage and pain,
Long lances, straight as sunbeams, tipped
　　With ruddy points, jerked through the
　　　crowd;
Bright axes rose awhile, and dipped,
　　And answering shrieks came high and loud.

But the red sun set, and the battle's din
Declined at length as the gloom fell in,
For the gunner's aim was no longer true,
And the pike-men scarce their foemen knew.

　　　　　Anon a crash—
　　　　　　A sudden stroke
　　　　A hush—a flash!
　　　　　　And the echoes woke
Through the circling hills as a cannon spoke!
Then a grapple and a clink of steel, and a hard
　　and hurried breath,
And an under growl of triumph, and a heavy
　　groan of death.

Still the darkness fell, and the fearless few
Who had braved a host, in the gloom withdrew·
But all night long from the blood-stained vale
Came the challenge stern, and the fitful wail,
And a busy hum on the eastern gale.

" What mean those songs and sounds of joy
That burst to-night from doomed Dunboy?"
The tired and wounded heroes cried,
As the castle gates were opened wide.
Surprised they saw within the hall
The ward assembled one and all,
The range of torches flaring red,
The cheer upon the tables spread,
The harper striking out his strains.
As if his strings were Ireland's chains—

" What news is here ?" with one loud voice
They asked, " that you can thus rejoice
While tread the Saxons on your shores,
Nay while they threat your very doors ?"
" Good news ", they answered ; " news to cheer
The hearts of all assembled here,
And all beside, who wish to see
The Saxon crushed, our country free.
But ere we speak it, let us know
How fared your onslaught on the foe " ?

" We scarce can tell ", the men replied ;
" But when our force they first espied,
Their cannon opened on our way
While not a gun had we to play
Upon their ranks ; yet on we rushed,
Into their midst our way we pushed,
And only ceased the unequal fight
When fell the darkling shades of night.
Behold the wounds we bear, and say
If lightly passed that sudden fray,
Or bid your wardens count and tell
Out of the few how many fell.—
But no—before a thought you turn
    On us—before a wound is drest,
Howe'er our flesh may pant and burn,
    First set our anxious minds at rest.—
Again we ask, what news of joy
What cheer, what hope for old Dunboy ?"

" Glad news", they answered : " more than hope,
   True aid, and proofs of love and care
From good King Philip and the Pope,
   Have reached our shores, are waiting near.
Within Kenmare's wood-bordered bay
Before our castle of Ardea
   A Spanish vessel rests her keel.
By holy men her deck is trod,
Owen Mac Egan, blest of God,
   And faithful friar Neale ;[10]
They come to ask our fortunes here,
To bid us boldly persevere
   For further aid will soon come o'er :
A force of fourteen thousand men
Was gathering for our service when
   They left the Spanish shore !
Even now they bring to our relief
Large sums in gold to every chief
   Who fights by gallant Donal's side.
They've brought us too across the brine
A store of gladdening, glorious wine,
   As ever Spain supplied !
They've brought us something to bestow
Upon our graceless Saxon foe,
   Though these the gift may welcome not,—
Some casks of powder good and strong,
To send into the ruffian throng,
   Some piles of iron shot !
Long may the good King Philip reign !
The glorious King of happy Spain,

And Ireland's friend—Hurra! Hurra!"
The words were echoed round about
The wounded men stood up to shout
 And ten times o'er to say—
" The King of Spain, the glorious King!
May Heaven prolong his life, and bring
 His heart new gladness day by day,
May glory and renown attend
The arts and arms of Ireland's friend,
 The King of Spain—Hurra!"

But when the gladsome shouts were o'er,
And converse might be held once more,
The wisest chieftains in the hall
Round Donal grouped, and said:
      " We all
Would urge you, Prince, that ere the morn
From out the bright'ning east is born
You reach Ardea, and promptly tell
Our worthy friends we greet them well.
Good Bishop Egan waits you there
His plans to shape, his gold to share.
King Philip bids him thus to do,
For much he trusts and hopes in you.
We'll guard Dunboy; though good your blade,
'Tis yours to bring us better aid;
Go wait the force that now must be
Fast speeding o'er the southern sea,
And bid them welcome when they stand
Arrayed upon our Irish strand;

Then as upon some wintry day
The rain-swelled river sweeps away
The matted drift the stream had tried
In vain to break or turn aside,
So rush you down the hills, and sweep
This Saxon rack into the deep.
Till then be ours the fiery task,
Though small may seem the force we ask,
One hundred men and forty-four
Our strength shall be,—we'll keep no more.—
But these, a brave and skilful few,
Shall do as much as men can do:
There's not a loop-hole in the wall
That shall not pour a rain of ball:
There's not an angle, nook, or joint,
From which some barrel, blade, or point,
Shall not project, to lay the foe
Who dares to venture near it, low".
"Good friends", said Donal: "I depart.
May Heaven protect each gallant heart
That beats before me here to-night,
And dares this Saxon horde to fight!
Mac Geohagan! your hand—your hand:
My honoured friend, the chief command
I leave to you till my return,
And well I know you'll bravely earn
From Donal thanks, from Ireland fame,
A patriot's meed, a hero's name.
Good soldiers all, and clansmen true
A brief, and but a brief, adieu!"

He said, and mounted on his steed
And dashed away at rapid speed;
Till at Knockoura's base again
He leaped to earth, he drew the rein
Around his arm, then quickly went
With light steps up the steep ascent.
But ere he made a single stride
Adown the mountain's further side,
He turned him round, and paused awhile
To see his Beara's morning smile.

The sun had risen, but dull clouds came
To bask before his face of flame,
And on the hills, still tinged with blue,
Broad stains of darker shadow threw.
The bay was dimmed with misty shade,
Like damp upon a polished blade ;
And o'er the villaged valleys hung
The gloom the passing night had flung.
But soon the strong sun rent away
Those tangling clouds of fleecy gray,
Set the slow drifting shreds on fire,
Climbed the blue air-fields high and higher,
And like a victor glad and free
Looked proudly down on land and sea.
A glory o'er the landscape spread,
The mist cleared off, the shadows fled,
Gay colours gladdened all the ground,
Out started hill and slope and mound,

And hut and hall, unseen before,
Now sparkled on the further shore.
As when an artist clears away
The gathered dust of many a day
From some old painting: sudden smiles
Some bright lake freck'd with golden isles,
Soft foliage gleams, the river foams,
Smooth fields spread out by sunny homes,
And in the foreground, sharp and clear,
Bright figures, men and maids, appear.
So looked the scene to Donal's sight
In that sweet gush of morning light.

Before him, framing in the bay,
A long brown rib of mountain lay;
Beyond again, a glittering spike
Of bright blue ocean, dagger-like,
Stretched far inland, and sea and sky
Were all beyond that met the eye.
That rough land nursed a race as stern,
Nursed boatmen bold and hardy kern,
And dauntless chieftains who would be
At home alike on land or sea.
But flowers of grace and beauty grew
Within its sheltered valleys too.
The wild rose of his heart had there
Sprung up and sweetened all the air:
With tender hands, with glistening eyes,
He gathered up the glorious prize,

And filled with love, with hope and joy,
He bore it to his own Dunboy!
Dunboy! He stroked his wrinkling brow
As thought contrasted then and now.
He sate him down a moment's space,
Within his hands he hid his face,
Then from the chambers of his brain
The grand old times trooped forth again,
And memory showed the happy day
He brought his Eileen o'er the bay.

Again from fleets of bannered boats
Sweet laughter rings, gay music floats.
Soft plashings of unnumbered oars,
Glad welcomes from the peopled shores,
Fond wishes, blessings, earnest prayers,
In one rich chorus, fill his ears,
And stir his heart; but sweeter still,
A deeper touch, a finer thrill,
The loved face blushing by his side
Reflects his looks of joy and pride!

They reach the shore; he leaps to land,
He takes his Eileen by the hand—
A storm, a storm of wild delight—
A whirl of blades and banners bright—
Faint gasps of music, well nigh drowned—
Within the sea of rougher sound—
Gay peasants dancing on the green—
Good cheer spread out the trees between—

Peace, plenty, mirth——

                    But, God! that roar
That shakes the hills!   His dream is o'er.

He started up, a glance he flung
    Upon the real scene below
A blue smoke round the turret hung
    Whence sped that death-bolt towards the foe,
And nigh the castle he could see
    The Saxon soldiers dotted round
In little knots of two and three
    To view the walls and mark the ground
For future conflict.

                    " Be it so",
The hero said.   " Full well I know
That did I choose to live a slave
    With bended neck and supple knees,
Even now one word of mine would save
My honoured home, my people brave,
    From foes and dangers such as these.
And she, my fond and gentle wife,
    Who shelters in Glengariffe now,
Might spend a tranquil, happy life,
Without one thought of bloody strife
    To cloud her sunny brow.
What—happy, said I?   Eileen dear,
    I did her wrong, but meant it not:
I know my love would mildly bear
The inward grief; would fondly share
    Her Donal's gloomy lot,

But happy? no, she could not be.
  Her brave good heart, though sorely tried,
Prefers to share those risks with me,
Accepts those toils unflinchingly,
Proud in her darkest hour to be
  A patriot's worthy bride!
Then be the issue what it may,
Upon this mountain top to-day,
  Beneath this arch of glittering blue,
By all on Earth my heart holds dear,
And all my hopes of Heaven, I swear
  ' To fight this struggle through!
Aye, to the last, though lost it be
Aye, while in all the isle I see
One shred of our good flag floating free
  With one hundred men beneath it,
I'll still be first in the holy toil
Our foes to slay, their plans to foil,
And my bones shall bleach on my native soil
  Or mine be the last sword sheathed.
Farewell, Dunboy".
       And he paced away,
But would frequent pause, and would musing say:
  " Yes, fearless hearts, as I ever found them—
One hundred men and forty-four
In those narrow halls—not a mortal more—[11]
  Four thousand foemen round them!

Another scene of mirth and light
Is all within Dunboy to-night.
The watches still are kept with care,
But feast and song are everywhere.
Beside the breeches of their guns
Sit groups of Beara's hardy sons,
And tell their deeds of war once more,
Or talk to-morrow's battle o'er.
The great hall like a casket shines,
The walls seem decked from diamond mines,
For burnished weapons catch the blaze,
And glint aside the glistening rays.
The oaken panels smooth and old
Flash in the light like sheets of gold,
And every carvéd point and curl
Seems silver streaked, or tipped with pearl!
Full oft before, that hall had been
A brilliant and a merry scene,
With yet a charm, an added light,
A sweetness wanted here to-night;
For then did Eileen with her lord
Make glad the room and head the board;
And Munster's brightest beauties were
From its best houses gathered there.
Daughters of fierce and haughty sires,
    Yet gentle maids, all smiles and sighs,
With nought that showed their fathers' fires,
    Save those bright sparkles in their eyes,

And nought to hint, in all their charms,
The strength within their brothers' arms.
Gone are those forms of light and grace
That oft had cheered the happy place,
But, like some building once o'ergrown
   With flowers that twined its columns
     round,
That stripped and bared into the stone,
  Is still a stately beauty found,
So looked the scene that evening, when
The hall was thronged with stalwart men;
When every arm could deal a blow
To lay the stoutest foeman low;
When every eye that sparkled there
Could range the gun or point the spear,
And every warrior, not alone
   For Ireland's cause could gladly die,
But first could lay beneath his own
   A foeman's corse whereon to lie.

"Come", said Mac Geohagan the brave,
  "Come, chieftains, friends, and comrades
    true,
We've had our councils calm and grave,
  Let's have our merry meeting too!
We know, when morning lights the land,
  Our foes, now well-prepared, will ope
Their guns from yonder rounded strand,
  Their battery from the mountain slope;[12]

And we, from out these good old walls,
    Shall send them hot and quick replies.
But ere the voice of battle calls
    Come, let the laugh and song arise!
I will be merry:—there has lain
    A grief within me, night and day,
For weary years, a ceaseless pain
    No human art could charm away:—
To-night—'tis strange—those sorrows turn
    To some new feeling like delight,
And dull cold shades that wrapt me, burn,
    Like sun clouds on the mountain height.
It is to-morrow's deadly strife
    That flings its ruddy rays before,
That warms the chilly stream of life,
    And stirs my heart with hope once more,—
With hope?—yes, hope I name it still—
    But, chieftains bold, my speech is long,
Come, Con O'Daly, prove your skill,
    Come, strike the harp!—a song, a song!

        Hurra, Hurra,
            Mac Geohagan
        Our noble chief"
            Cried every man
        "Our Captain good and true!"

Upon the wall the bright arms shivered
As tables, roof, and flooring quivered,

The flags around the room depending
Stirred in the storm of sound ascending,
The clansmen filled their goblets flowing
And set the shout once more agoing—

> " Hurra, Hurra,
>   Mac Geohagan,
> The trusted chief
>   Of Donal's clan,
> Mac Geohagan abu!"

Before the din had died away
The prelude of O'Daly's lay
Came on the ear in silvery tinklings,
Strong wild gusts, and starry sprinklings,
Growing louder, fuller, clearer,
As down sat cheerer after cheerer,
'Till amidst the listening throng
    Every voice to silence hushed,
Thus his new-made tune and song
    Like a rain-swelled river rushed.

I.

The foemen are round us to-day,
            To-day ;
The Saxons are round us to-day,
    With their merciless bands
    Come to ravage our lands,
To plunder, to burn, and to slay !
    Let us rise in our might,
    Let us rush to the fight,

And crush them or chase them away—
　　　　　　　Hurra!
Let us crush them or chase them away!

II.

They come like the wolf on his prey
　　　　　　　To day,
To rend and to tear—if they may:
　　They shall break like the shock
　　Of the waves on the rock
That is moveless abroad in the bay!
　　Even so the thin flood
　　Of their Sassanach blood
Shall be spirted and washed into spray,
　　　　　　　Hurra!
Round the brave men of Beara to-day.

III.

We are one to their twenty, they say,
　　　　　　　To-day;
We are one against twenty, they say—
　　But to count man for man
　　Of O'Sullivan's clan
With their clouts, is to count them in play!
　　They shall soon know our worth
　　When our men sally forth
Like lightnings unloosed, to the fray,
　　　　　　　Hurra!
To cleave them or chase them away!

The men applauded loud and long,
They praised the music and the song,
   "Well done! well done"! they cried;
"O'Daly, could we only do
Our parts as yours is done by you,
We'd soon mow down this English crew,
   And sweep them to the tide!
Ha-ha! ha-ha!—well done, old Con,
No fire from out your veins is gone,
   Although your head be white as snow;
Your blood is hot, your ear is fine,
Your touch upon the silver twine
Is clear and fresh, and sounds divine
   Like sweet wild winds around you blow,
     Till passion-stirred,
     Such storms are heard,
As that which burst awhile ago".

"Well done O'Daly, right well done—
My instrument—a six-feet gun,
   Shall sound its notes to-morrow morn",
Said tall Hugh Roe, who loved a fight
And liked a joke; a merry wight
With thick red beard and eyes of light,
   And voice that rung like hunting horn.

"Come", said the revellers, "merry Hugh,
Let's have your own old song from you:
   We've heard it twenty times before—
You'll sing it oft, we trust, again

To laughing maids and merry men,
But, lest we may not hear it then,
　　Give us the rhyme once more".
Loud laughed tall Hugh, and then he swung
His head in time, while thus he sung :—

I.

My name is Hugh Roe,
And not long, you must know,
　　Had my friends seen my presence exciting,
When my spirit broke out,
And I proved beyond doubt,
　　I was born with a fancy for fighting.

II.

From nurse-maids to men
Have I battled since then :
　　All over the isle I've been ranging :
And strifes that were tough
And furious enough,
　　Have I shared, but my taste is unchanging.

III.

It is only the right
I espouse in the fight,
　　I aid no ill cause whatsoever ;
But there's plenty of wrong
In this world, on my song,
　　To keep a man fighting for ever.

IV.

And who needs to ask
For a warrior's task,
  Whose heart has one throb for his sire-land,
While Sassanach clowns
Waste the fields and the towns,
  And strive to be masters of Ireland!

V.

For a soldier like me,
What the ending must be,
  I know as if clearly foreshown it;
When that ending comes round,
I'll not grieve, I'll be bound,
  And I'll ask no one else to bemoan it.

VI.

But I hope that my name
In our annals of fame
  Will be set in a small piece of writing,[13]
Saying "Then, and just so,
Fell the gallant Hugh Roe,
  Who was born with a fancy for fighting".

"Well done, Hugh! right well sung, Hugh!"
The room re-echoed through and through.
" His words are truth", one clansman cried;
"His foes would own it", one replied;

4

" I've seen him in the deadly strife
With every blow blot out a life;
I've heard the crash of cloven bones,
I've heard the growl of heart-wrung groans,
Go with him as he cleaved his way
Right through the thickest of the fray".

"No wonder", one remarked; " but few
Can boast of arms like those of Hugh.
I've seen their strength one evening, when
He played with Carbery's hardiest men :
Each tried in vain to lift a block
Of stone from off a neighbouring rock :
He raised it with a quiet grace
Up to his knees, his hips, his face,
Then flung it off so far away
That some around were heard to say
'Twould take a right good powder blast
To give it such another cast".

" And I", another said, " have seen
Him snap an ash limb tough and green
Between his hands with seeming ease,
Which others strained across their knees
And could not break.   But see his wrist,
The breadth across his rugged fist—
Why let him take into his own
An arm of average flesh and bone,—
He'd turn it like a woollen twist !

But hush! no more of strong-limbed Hugh;
They ask a song of Dermod Dhu,
Who loves, as all Berehaven knows,
   The prettiest maid in half the land,
Yet comes to crush his country's foes
   Before he takes her snowy hand.
Hush, hush, good friends, I would not choose,
When he begins to sing, to lose
   A single soft, delicious note,
For nature in some curious start
Gave Dermod, with a manly heart,
   A woman's dainty lips and throat".
So spoke the men themselves among
'Till Dermod thus sang out his song:—

I.

Beneath a mountain rough and hoary
   Lies a valley fair to view,
A river, like an olden story,
   Softly winds and murmurs through.
     There she dwells, my Una dear,
      Una, dear as life to me,
       Una of the golden hair,
        White-necked Una óg machree.*

II.

In that valley flowers are springing
   All the rounding months along;
Birds upon the boughs are singing
   One unending happy song.

* *Anglice*—White-necked young Una of my heart.

Little may be my surprise—
   Una day by day they see,
    Una of the bright blue eyes,
        Darling Una óg machree.

III.

So my thoughts are full of flowers,
   So my heart with song runs o'er,
While I dream of happy hours,
   By that river's winding shore.
    Happy with my Una dear,
     Una dear as life to me,
      Una ever fond and fair,
        Bright-eyed Una óg machree.

Who stalks like a spectre right into the hall,
Why start up the chiefs and the revellers all?
Whence comes he—with visage all pale, save
   those streaks
Of red gaping wounds on his forehead and cheeks?
Whence comes he?—he presses his hand on his
   side,
Where the folds of his clothing with crimson are
   dyed?
His eyes for a moment are darkened with pain,
And his head droops aside, but he rallies again.
They bear him along to a couch like a mound,
Of brightest hued silks flung in heaps to the
   ground,

Soft cushions they push 'neath his shoulders and
    hips,
And they pour the red wine through his colour-
    less lips ;
He motions his thanks with his hands and his eyes,
And thus to their queries at length he replies :—

Two days ago, friends,
Two days ago,
In Dursey island
We fought the foe.

But forty men
In the forts were we,
They came a hundred
And fifty-three.

On our northmost fort
First their fury fell ;
We fought them long,
And we fought them well ;
Even they must own
That we fought them well.

But their guns were many,
And ours were few ;
And a stronger fort
Was the south, we knew—
To our southern fort
Then our men withdrew.

And again we fought them,
Both long and well:
That the fight was fierce
Even they must tell;
For fast their soldiers
Before us fell.

Each man we lost
Cost the Saxons two,
But they could spare them—
Their bloody crew
Were thrice our number—
What could we do?

When further contest
Was all in vain,
When our guns were broken,
Our captains slain,
And no help was near us
On isle or main—

Our men surrendered,
And doing so
Believed they dealt
With a gallant foe.—
How fared they after
You soon shall know.

Within their camp,
Only yesterday,

One after one
Did they foully slay.
Their blood yet clots
On the yellow clay.

They thought me dead, friends,
They thought me dead,
As I lay and moved
Neither hands nor head,
Though the friends I loved
Were my gory bed.

But when night fell dark
And the sentries slept,
O'er the cold wet grass
From their camp I crept.

And I made my way
To the castle door.
Good friends, I faint,
I can speak no more.

"Comrades!" Mac Geohagan exclaimed,
While like red fires his large eyes flamed—
"Though sad our wounded brother's tale,
Let no stout heart amongst you quail;
For though we may not hence retire
  To Dursey's forts, now battered low,

Yet could we cross the belt of fire
That wraps us round, who would desire
   From our dear castle now to go?
And if our comrades brave are slain,
If honour's, mercy's pleas were vain,
Let this but urge us on again
   To smite so base, so false a foe!"

"Aye", cried the soldiers, "let us feel
   The spirits of our friends are here,
To nerve our hearts, to point our steel,
   To tell us how to strike and where!
Yes, let us deem the castle now
   Dunboy and Dursey both in one,
And only think and labour how
   With axe and sword, with pike and gun,
   The double work may best be done"—

"God save you, soldiers", said the priest
   As slow he strode into the room—
   "The stars die out, fast fades the gloom,
And morn is blushing in the east.

"I told my beads the live-long night
   And watched as well as prayed for you,
   For well by certain signs I knew,
That morn would bring the bloody fight.

"Soon loud shall burst the battle note—
   I've seen them feed each levelled gun,

Crowd round the piece awhile, and run
The ball into its iron throat.

"To arms, good friends, without delay—
  Ha! see that vivid, blinding flash!
  Hark, hear that roar—that sudden crash!
And hear again, their loud huzza!

" Haste, soldiers, each unto his post—
  I wish you triumph, glory, fame,
  I bless you in the potent name
Of Father, Son, and Holy Ghost!"

———

The skies were red with morning light
  When the English guns commenced to play,
From batteries, planted through the night,
  At seven score yards from the walls away.
Thick dykes stood round the castle's base,
  Hurriedly raised since the Saxons came,
But high on the building's western face
  Was the chosen point of the gunners' aim.

One after one,
Each massive gun
Roared, and anon
  Crashed all together—

Echoed the sound
Through the hills around
Like a thunder peal in stormy weather!

Hour after hour,
The iron shower
Rained on the tower
  That groaned and rumbled—
Ball after ball
Eat through the wall,
Till the turret tottered, slipped, and tumbled!

Down with a crash on the vault below;
  Down was the castle's best gun hurried,
In fell the vault with the mighty blow,
  And brave men deep in the wreck were buried.

Then lower on the castle's side
  The English turned their cannon all;
Again the gray old pile was plied
  With a steady hail of racking ball—

Gun after gun,
Till hours had run,
And the blinding sun
  In the south was flashing—
The big stones split,
As the bullets hit,
And the splinters flew from the granite crashing!

Firm and tough
Was the building stuff
That torn, and rough,
   So long impended—
A flash! a roar!
One dull stroke more,
And the whole field shook as the mass descended!

Then loud the Saxons' shout arose,
   They waved their flags with frantic joy:
"Hurra", they cried, "thus die our foes,
   Thus falls the famed Dunboy!"

Forth from the ruined building came
A soldier whose white flag would claim
Exception from the gunner's aim.

His peaceful errand bent to do,
The Saxon camp he marched unto,
And asked to speak with Lord Carew.

"Aye, let the rebel pass to me"
The wily chief said "we shall see
What may his comrades' thinkings be.

"But when we've heard his story, then,
Be yours the care, my trusty men,
He never sees Dunboy again.

Before him was the envoy led,
His white flag drooping o'er his head ;
He gravely bowed, and thus he said :

"My comrades send me, Lord Carew,
With peaceful offers unto you,
As brave men in their strait may do.

"With yours compared, their force is small,
Their guns are few ; wall after wall
Before your stronger fire must fall.

"Yet think they even they may say,
For every man your force might slay
Your army with a life would pay.

"With hearts for either fortune steeled,
They offer now in peace to yield
The castle and the battle field,

"If, with their arms and colours, they
Shall all be free to take their way
Where'er they please, from hence to-day".

"No" said Carew, "in sooth not so,
We offered terms ere yet a blow
Was interchanged, some weeks ago.

"You scorned them then, and by my vow,
No peace, no truce shall we allow
Howe'er you pray or parley now.

" And mark !—we saw you hither press,
And wave your sign of peacefulness,
Yet fired your guns no shot the less.

" Your cannon flashed your flag to mock,
Your balls came in with stroke and shock—
Ho, Marshall ! bear him to the block !"

The trumpets brayed ! the army stirred,
    And quick assumed the battle build,
While summoned by that warning word
    The breach with Beara's soldiers filled.
Full in the front stood tall Hugh Roe,
    Who smiled and cheered his gallant
        band,
He swung his long sword to and fro
And freed his elbows for the blow
With which he meant to greet the foe
    That now were tramping near at hand.
The trumpets sounded ! onward pressed
    The English ranks—a shout, a screech,
Told when the men were breast to breast
    And grappled in the deadly breach !

Glaring in each other's faces, hissing in each
    other's ears,
Searching for the mortal places where to plant
    their shining spears,

C

Striking in with sudden lunges, with the sword
  blade deftly sloped,
Starting forth with forceful plunges when the
  ranks a moment ope'd;
Panting, straining, loud complaining, as the wells
  of life were found,
And the bright red tide came raining quickly on
  the dusty mound,
Grunting gladly, cheering madly, answering with
  a bitter yell,
When some fierce hard-striking foeman caught
  the deadly wound and fell;
Beaten backward for a moment, pressing on again
  in haste,
All the crumbling dust beneath them trampling
  into bloody paste—
So they fought the murderous combat, while the
  red-faced sun looked down
From between his crimson curtains on the landscape with a frown,
Deepening till the hills seemed risen freshly from
  some purple flood,
And the tranquil sea below them looked a flowing bath of blood.

Wounded thrice with musket bullets, scarred by
  keen and ready blades,
Captain Kirton held the passage, calling loud for
  English aids.

Mewtas answered to the summons, rushing forward
  with a cheer,
Hurling fresh and eager forces on the gallant
  men of Beare;
Well they met them; added vigor into every blow
  they flung,
Quicker now their swords descended, deeper now
  their pike points stung;
To and fro throughout the battle ranged the brave
  Mac Geohagan,
Cheering on his gallant soldiers, watching well
  his foemen's plan,
Rushing when the need was greatest madly for-
  ward to the front,
Often for a time sustaining all alone the battle's
  brunt.
By the eddying of the combat, circling, surging,
  one might know
Where the tide was breaking wildly on that
  rugged rock, Hugh Roe.
Oft his blood-stained blade was lifted, but the
  eye could only see
In the air a bright red circle, coming, going
  suddenly,
As one sees when playful children twirl a fire-
  tipp'd stick at night,
And the vision catches only one bright band of
  ruddy light.
Strong limbed Hugh! a score of foemen thought
  their might but matched in him,

And he seemed to take the honour with a pleasure
wild and grim,
Earning well the high opinion as his vengeful
blade he plied
And from out the group he wrought on, foemen
staggered, dropped, and died.

Still the bloody gap was holden by the castle's
gallant few,
Loud again the trumpets sounded for the troop
of Lord Carew;
Fast into the breach they flooded, and before the
gathered strength,
Far outnumbered, thrice o'erpowered, Beara's
men gave way at length;
Slowly yielding 'twixt the buildings raised around
the castle's base,
Inch by inch the ground disputing, till they
reached a sheltered space
Where the cannon of their foemen raked no more
their little band,
And the fight was closer, fiercer—man to man
and hand to hand.

Long within that narrow passage was the furious
strife maintained,
Hours of bloody toil passed over, not a step the
Saxons gained;
Nought availed their greater numbers, in the
narrow frontage there,

Beara's sturdy men presented sword for sword
and spear for spear.

Quickly fell the foremost foemen; pressed the
forces closer yet,

Wearing, grinding down each other at the edges
where they met.

Never paused the strife a moment, till a sharp
and sudden cheer

Made the tired and baffled Saxons look around
and up with fear,

High upon the ruined castle, standing on the
broken wall,

Armed with many a weighty missile, jagged stone
and iron ball,

Stood a range of Irish soldiers—soon into the
narrow pass

Flung they down their ponderous weapons on the
solid Saxon mass,

Crushing strongest men like stubble, beating gaps
into the crowd,

That like helpless things could only shiver, shriek,
and howl aloud.

On the castle's ragged outline, perched upon its
highest part,

Bold O'Moore[15] was seen to labour, striving hard
with all his heart:

Fragments from the wall he rooted, swung them
upward to his teeth,

Hissed and cast them fiercely from him on the
groaning ranks beneath,

Shouting, singing, dancing wildly, as he saw the
    weighty stones
Reach the earth and drive before them mangled
    flesh and shattered bones ;
Still the patient Saxons suffered, hoping strong
    reliefs were near,
For they knew their men were seeking entrance
    through the castle's rear.
And ere long their hopes were answered ; fast
    their regiments hurried through,
Sought and found the narrow passage held by
    Beara's fearless few.
Gallant Hugh ! they hastened towards him, soon
    a dozen rays of steel
In his manly heart were buried like the spokes
    within a wheel ;
Up they rushed into the ruin—Ha, those soldiers
    on the wall—
Never more shall these be flinging jagged stone
    or iron ball ;
Down they dragged them, stabbed and clove
    them, saw their death wounds doubly sure,
Turned to wreak their direst vengeance on their
    deadliest foe O'Moore,
But he sprung from off the ruin ; ere he touched
    the bloody ground
Saxon spears ran redly through him and a speedier
    death was found.
Downward from the rooms they hastened, for
    despite the force below,

Saw they sallying from the castle forty of the
    Irish foe,
Hastening whither? where was shelter? short the
    space they had to flee,
English troops were close beside them, straight
    before them spread the sea;
Caught between the closing regiments, soon the
    little band was crushed,
But a few strong men escaping, thence into the
    water rushed;
Swam, with clinging clothes encumbered, boldly
    for the island's shore,
Though the point that jutted nearest, distant lay
    a mile or more;
Slowly o'er the waveless water glided on each
    rugged head,
But the sounds of oars came to them ere one
    fourth their course was sped;
Fast came up the boats pursuing, from each bow
    and o'er the side
Saxon soldiers drove their lances through the
    swimmers in the tide;
One by one beneath the surface dipped the heads
    and disappeared,
Loud the troops on shore applauded, loud the
    brutal boatmen cheered;
Scarce a token of the slaughter in a minute more
    remained
Save where'er the dull green water with a ruddy
    hue was stained,

Save that glancing sharply downward, bloody
    streaks were seen to grow
Like long strings of purple sea-weed branching
    from each corse below;
Save that when the boats returned, thin red lines
    of human gore
Marked their sides with wavy outlines, circled
    round each clumsy oar.

Once again the English captains ordered on a
    new assault,
Ere the night to crush the clansmen still disputing
    hall and vault.
Onward pressed the Saxon forces, hoarsely cheer-
    ing as they dashed
Hard upon their desperate foemen while their
    helping cannon crashed:
Never quailed the patriot soldiers; hideous now
    with dust and blood,
Plying well their blunted weapons, strong in their
    despair they stood,
Checking oft their swarming foemen—but despite
    of stop and stay,
Still the crowding English regiments slowly, surely,
    won their way.
Short the space they had to traverse, yet the time
    was told by hours
Ere they planted on the ruin flags that waved
    like gaudy flowers.

Joyful leaped the English soldiers, burst a cheer
  from every throat,
When they saw their blood-stained banners o'er
  the hard won capture float.
But their task not yet was ended; in a moment
  more they found
Their unyielding foes descended to the cellars
  underground,
Vainly did they strive to follow down those
  narrow stairs of stone,
Every man who ventured forward tumbled inward
  with a groan!
Hold! cried out the wearied captains to their
  tired and wounded men,
Hold! we rest till dawns the morning; we shall
  rout the rebels then.
Set a guard above the cellars, watch the place
  with sword and fire,
Let the force no longer needed to their canvas
  quick retire!

  Spoke a voice from far below,
  "Saxon soldiers! listen ho!
  Brave men fight, but never do
  Murder on a vanquished few:
  Here we yield, we end the strife,
  Claiming, asking, only life".

  "Irish rebels, beaten foe",
  Spoke the victors, "listen, ho!

At our mercy simply yield,
We are masters of the field.
In our hands we hold your fate
Vainly now of terms you prate".

Spoke the voices from below,
"Never, never: well we know,
Taught by black and bloody scenes,
What your Saxon mercy means.
If our blood must glut your hate,
Take it at a dearer rate".

"Soldiers!" cried the Saxon captains, "watch
   the place through midnight's gloom:
If they yield not ere the morning, their retreat
   becomes their tomb".

But seventy men and six, of those
   Who dared four thousand to the fight,
When morning o'er Dunboy arose,
   Beneath the ruin grouped at night.
And these were weary, wounded, weak,
   Some, one might see, would droop and die
Before another rosy streak
   Of morning touched the eastern sky.

The white haired bard who proudly sung
   While last night's hours on light wings flew,
Now bent above his harp unstrung,
   His heart unstrung and shattered too.
And there upon the moist cold ground
   Mac Geohagan low moaning lay,
While forth from many a crimson wound
   His life blood dripped and ebbed away.
Many a stout limbed son of Beare,
   A giant in his strength that morn,
Lay wearied, faint, and wounded there,
   Weak as an infant newly born.
Some just could struggle through the task
   Across the room to limp or crawl,
By groping on from cask to cask,
   And steadying by the cellar wall.
Not one was there unmarked with gore,
   With scar and bruise, with blood and dust,
No weapon on the ground but bore
   Some crimson stain or purple crust.

" Friends", said the warrior priest, "though ill
I speak their Saxon jargon, still,
Methinks were I but face to face
With their stern chief to plead our case,
My words might have sufficient art
To reach and touch his cruel heart.
In other lands 'twas mine to see
Brave soldiers flushed with victory,

To hear full oft' addressed to those
The fair appeal of vanquished foes,
And, whatsoe'er the battle's heat,
Howe'er his heart might burn and beat,
I've seen the conquering soldier stand,
And sudden stay his vengeful hand,
When as he swung his blade in air,
The yielding foeman shouted 'spare!'
Yes; battles won and lost I've seen;
Vanquished and victor have I been,
I, Dominick Collins: at the head
Of gallant troops of horse I've sped;
Firm in my hand the trusty lance
Grasped for the Holy League of France—[16]
And borne me—so I hope at least—
As fits a soldier and a priest.
I will confront our Saxon foes,
Perhaps in one brief hour to close
The life I care not to prolong
In this wild world of sin and wrong;
But yet perhaps some good to do,
To win the terms you seek for you.
Full well I know that one and all
As little care what fate befal,
Yet well may I be found the first
To hope the best and brave the worst".

Then said the soldiers: "Be it so,
But bless us, Father, ere you go.

Light is the soldier's heart, who feels
   That, howsoe'er war's thunders roll,
Whate'er the fate red battle deals,
   No ills can reach his sinless soul;
Who in the wildest danger sees
   The path to win the world's renown,
His country's thanks, or, failing these,
   Death, and with death a brighter crown.
Bless us, good Father, bless us all;
To-morrow let what may befal".

He bless'd them all, and begged their pray'rs,
Then mounted up the narrow stairs.
Slow, as if half resolved he stept,
   Till on the topmost stone at last,
One bitter burst of grief he wept,
   Then forth into the air he passed.

The cellar gloom was damp and chill;
'Tis true the night was short, but still
Those few brief hours, the soldiers said,
A cheerier time might well be made.
They struck their flints and quickly raised
A merry fire that cracked and blazed,
They fed the flame with logs of pine
Wet with strong usquebaugh and wine;
Unto the warmth the strongest men
Brought up their weaker friends, and then
From the rich plenty round them stored,
That oft had decked a gayer board,

Drew forth and gave, with kindly speech,
Good cheer around to all and each
Who still could drain a cup or two,
To Ireland and her soldiers true.
But generous drinks and grateful food,
To glad the heart and warm the blood,
Were not the only stores that lay
Around them heaped and stowed away.
Not long erect on Irish land
Could princely hall or castle stand,
Which had, close by its basement stone,
But corn and wines and meats alone,
And held not full supplies for those
Who came the way as friends or foes.
By that deep cellar's walls were found
Stout barrels trebly hooped and bound,
They held—not fare to cheer and brace
The huntsman weary of the chase,
They were not wells whose taste would move
The lips to song, the heart to love—
Beneath their lids so closely kept,
A fierce, a mighty giant slept;
One touch of fire would break the spell,
And raise from out each fragile shell
A dazzling shape, that with a flash—
A thunder roar—a sudden crash—
Would crush and kill, would scorch and burn,
Cast down, uproot, and overturn,
Would scatter wreck and death around,
Then pass from off the blackened ground

As quickly to the trembling air,
And on the instant vanish there!
Unto the centre of the floor
One barrel from that dreadful store,
The soldiers moved, and quick undid
The fastenings of its heavy lid,
But loosely on the dull black grain
Laid the thick covers down again,
Then turned to spend the passing night
As well and gaily as they might.

"Soldiers!" in accents faint and weak,
Mac Geohagan was heard to speak :—
"Amid the battle's crash and heat
I've watched you well, and now 'tis meet
That ere my lips are closed for aye,
I own your gallant deeds, and say,
That well you've borne the bloody day.
The ruined pile above will stand,
A sign to all who tread the land,
That by no brief assault was won
The fight that wrecked this stout old Dun ;
That here, these ragged walls among,
Defenders brave, assailants strong,
In deadly combat battled long!
God rest the dead, the brave and true,
But, living comrades, what of you?
In one brief hour, as all must know,
Above our heads will swarm the foe—

If still my brave men's lives they ask,
If still they crave their bloody task,
Then, comrades, then—the powder cask!
Aha! about my heart I feel
A hand as hard and cold as steel,
And yet, despite the mortal pain
A glory bathes my dying brain!—
O'Daly! touch my favourite string,
Sweet thoughts in wildering music fling,
Upon my heart: O'Daly, sing!"

"A shattered harp is mine to-night",
    O'Daly said, "for even I,
When hotly raged the unequal fight,
And red blood flowed before my sight,
    Could not stand idly by.
I scarcely thought this withered arm
Could work the cursed brood such harm,
But yet beneath the weights I hurled,
    More than one hateful Saxon hound
Howled out with pain, bowed down and curled,
    And rolled upon the bloody ground.
But while I stood upon the wall
    Some marksman keen my post espied,
Ere long a well aimed musket ball
    Ripped up the flesh along my side,
And glancing struck the harp I laid
    Not far away.   Our songs are o'er,
My harp, my much-loved harp, I said;
    Dunboy will hear thy strains no more!

But yet a few deep chords remain,
   I'll wake the tones though faint they be,
One old air haunts my darkening brain—
   And thus I sing, my chief, for thee.

I.

'Tis bitter news for Bantry, 'tis gloomy news for
   Beare,
'Tis mournful news for Ireland, the grief that
   smites us here:
Mavrone, mavrone, our tribes will groan, and
   own the weight of woe,
As white lips say, " Beside the bay Dunboy is
   lying low".

II.

No wonder sighs and sobs should rise ; no wonder
   tears should run ;
No wonder Erin dear should weep, as a mother
   weeps her son ;
'Neath many a loss and heavy cross 'twas her's
   to bend and bow,
But some were bliss and joy to this that breaks
   her fond heart now.

III.

But, good and gallant clansmen, enough, enough
   for you,
You've fought the fight for Ireland's right, as
   Ireland's sons should do.

God will decree what's yet to be, but pray, dear
    clansmen, pray,
That soon His hand may raise our land, and
    chase her foes away.

IV.

Home of my race, my native place, green isle,
    I've loved thee long;
Low at thy feet, I've hymned thee, sweet, and laid
    my gift of song;
But joy more true I never knew, than now, a gra
    machree,
When this red flood of living blood flows from
    my heart for thee.

The song is hushed, the listeners speak,
Even dying men, bowed down and weak,
A moment raise their heads to say,
The bard ne'er sung a sweeter lay.
But one whose praise was ever dear
As blessings to the harper's ear,
Speaks not, moves not—what can it be?
They hasten to their chief to see—
He lives! he lives; he is not dead,
His noble spirit has not fled,
Though like a corse the hero lies
With lips relaxed and closéd eyes.
They lay his massive frame at ease,
His head upon a soldier's knees;

They loose the gun and sword belts wound
His manly breast and body round,
Then, lest the Saxon troops come on,
And find their ordered valour gone,
To Taylor, ever wise and brave,
The chief command with greetings gave.
Nor could the faithful clansmen's voice
Have spoken out a better choice.
His was a heart that never knew
A moment's fear, but firmer grew
When danger near and nearer came,
And death's keen dart seemed sure of aim.
His form, of more than middle height,
Stood like a poplar straight and slight;
His face was pale, his cheeks were deep,
The bones alone would seem to keep
Their sides apart; his gray eyes seemed
To light a brain that ever dreamed;
His yellow hair was loosely thrown
From off the lofty plate of bone ·
That o'er them stood: He looked a man
Steady of purpose, slow to plan,
But sure to act, and aye abide
By that his will should once decide.
He took the post they called him to:
Its duties now were plain and few:
He pushed a seat across the floor,
And placed it by the powder store;
He sate him calmly down, and bid
The soldiers lift the loosened lid;

Soon as the Saxons' tramp came near,
  He firmly grasped a burning brand.
He listened with an anxious ear,
  And held the red light in his hand,
Then when their haughty summons broke
The silence, to his men he spoke :—

"Soldiers, the hour for strife is past,
The fight is fought, the die is cast.
Yield ye who will.   I set ye free ;
Let those who choose remain with me ;
But which are braver, none may say,
The men who leave, or those who stay,—
All fought the hard fight yesterday.
Yield ye who will : I still remain,
Once more, though well I know in vain,
  Our last night's terms of peace to ask.
Should they but mock my words again,
  To answer with the powder cask.

A moment's pause, and twenty-three
  Sore wounded men together came,
Spoke to their comrades mournfully,
  And bowed their heads, as if in shame,
Then slowly climbed the bloody stair,
Moved out into the morning air,
  Still with the night dews chill and damp,
Marched straight across the well known ground,
And in a minute more were bound
  In chains within the Saxon camp.

Another pause, and from the few
Within the gloomy vault, withdrew
Three war worn men, Spain's worthy sons,
Who bravely worked the castle guns,
And spurned the bribes Carew would pay
To win them from their posts away.
Not less their proud hearts' bitter grief,
   That there were guns to work no more,
For Spanish king or Irish chief,
'Gainst Saxon dogs of unbelief,
   On Irish sea or shore.

Again the Saxons shouted, "Ho!
Irish rebels still below,
Yield, or we batter down a wall
Above your heads, and one and all
Imprisoned in the vault remain
And soon for exit howl in vain".

"Promise life unto my men",
Taylor said: "we yield but then.
Still refuse, and with the brand
Brightly flaming in my hand,
Friends and foes at once shall I
Hurl in one blast tow'rds the sky".[17]

The Saxons left with curse and frown,
   Again their cannon redly flashed,
   Their huge balls through the ruin crashed,
And fast the old walls wasted down.

But see, from midst the dusty drifts
A figure comes, his hand he lifts
Above his head, and drawing near
His shouted words the English hear :—

"We yield! we yield! we strive no more,
Our arms are piled on the cellar floor.
Taylor, our captain, murmurs yet,
But we hush his voice with plea and threat.
Enter; the clansmen round you lying
Will strike no more; are dead or dying".

Into the vault the Saxons ran :
   The voices and the tramp of feet
Aroused the chief Mac Geohagan,
   Whose heart had well nigh ceased to beat.
With hard wild stare he looked around,—
   Were these the Saxons near him ? what !—
His gallant men disarmed and bound?
   He tottered to the flames and caught
A glowing ember in his hand,
   Then towards the cask held on his way.
The English soldiers saw the brand,
   And rushed in front his course to stay;
Their captain, Power, forward flew,
   And grasped the dying hero fast,
The while another of the crew,
His bloody weapon through and through
   The noble chieftain's body passed.

Slow dripped the blood; that heart had nigh,
Before the cruel deed, run dry;
   But ere his gallant spirit fled,
Lord Thomond caught the chieftain's eye,
   And thus with dying breath he said :—

"Ha! Earl, you'll own I told you true
   When on the island's side we met;
The words should still be known to you,
   I can recall them even yet—
'No English troops shall ever find
A shelter from the rain and wind;
No English preacher ever raise
A canting hymn in England's praise;
No English council ever prate
The weal or woe of England's state;
Nor Irish slave one hour enjoy,
Beneath the roof of proud Dunboy'.
I spoke you thus, and, traitor, tell,
Have I not kept my promise well?

"Donal and Eileen! yes, I see,
You're here to laugh and sing with me.
Strike up, O'Daly! prove your skill!
What! Why is all so cold and still?
So still and dark! Where am I? Where?
Donal and Eileen! No one near!
Ah! yes, I know. Dunboy, good bye!
God take my soul! I die, I die!"

That eve within the Saxon's camp,
   The headman's strokes continued long.
With a steady champ, like a measured tramp,
   For the clansmen's bones were stout and strong."

————

Four days from thence the Saxon troops,
   Their guns and stores had stowed away
   Into their ships; to-morrow they
   Would cross again the heaving bay.
And wherefore stood those watchful groups
On board upon the vessels' poops,
   On shore on many a rocky height,
   And towards the ruin turned their sight?

    The outworks stand,
      And some walls are high,
    Though a useless heap
      As they meet the eye.
    Even these must fall,
      The Saxons swear:
    Each work and wall,
    They shall level all,
      Ere they sail from Beare.

The train is laid to the powder store,
The fire creeps on—in a moment more
The flame leaps forth with a hoarse dull roar,

Dazzling the eye
  With a wildering light,
That makes the noon sky
  Look black as night!
The flash is passed; a smoky pall
  Hides for a time the wreck around,
While fragments of the broken wall,
And high-hurled stones, returning, fall
    On the trembling ground
      With a heavy crash;
    Into the sea
,   With a noisy plash.
    The once green bank
      With the wreck is cumbered;
    With beam and plank
      Is the blue tide lumbered.
The dust drifts by, the smoke clouds sever,
      But no castle now
      Shows its haughty brow,
Dunboy is swept from the earth for ever.

———

He saw the flash, he heard the sound,
  As o'er Knockoura's hill he came;
He shrieked and made a sudden bound,
  As if his heart had felt the flame.

As if some huge and heavy stone,
Forth from the blazing ruin thrown,
  Had struck him down, to earth he fell;
A shudder, and a fitful groan,
  Awhile were all the signs to tell
That through the prostrate body ran
The hot blood of a living man.

He rose again, he gazed about,
  His eyes beheld Dunboy no more;
The very walls were blotted out—
He scarcely knew the place, without
  That building by the shore.
The sea, the hills, seemed something strange,
So great, so sad, the sudden change,
  In one destructive moment wrought;
He sate him down a moment's space,
Within his hands he hid his face,
Again his mind was with the past,—
The day he saw that valley last
  Was glowing in his thought.
But from the long day-dream he broke,
And oft-used words again he spoke :—

" Aye, be the issue what it may,
On this hill-side again to-day,
  I pledge my sacred vow anew.
By all on Earth my heart holds dear,
And all my hopes of Heaven, I swear
  To fight this struggle through.

To fight it through, though well I see
  Few are the hopes that now remain
To you, my native land, or me;
  Our forts are fallen, our chiefs are slain,
And men of Irish blood and birth
  Are stooping down to vile disgrace,
Showing that scandal to the Earth,
  The rotting of a noble race.
Crushed into slaves are royal tribes,
  High chieftains fight for Saxon pay,
The sons of kings take foreign bribes,
  . Brothers their brothers' blood betray,
And clan on clan works ruin, while
The common foe wins all the isle.
Yet while in all the land I see
One shred of our good flag floating free,
  With a hundred men beneath it,
I'll still be first in the holy toil,
Our foes to slay, their plans to foil;
My bones shall bleach on my native soil,
  Or mine be the last sword sheathed!"

So spoke the chief, and well he kept
  His oft' repeated promise true;
Though Desmond, hill and vale, was swept
  By Wilmot, Thomond, and Carew;
Yet with a brave and desperate band,
That flocked to him from half the land,

He still defied the Saxons' might,
Dashed on their outposts day and night,
And many a stately keep and dun,
Back from their Irish allies won;[19]
Yet like a steady tide arose,
The triumph of his Saxon foes,
And from his side, day after day,
Some new support was swept away.
Brave Tirrell, filled with wide despair,
Moved northward from the hills of Beare,
And Burke, when all looked darker yet
From Donal parted with regret.
One gallant chief, Iraeti's lord,
  O'Connor Kerry, still remained,
And held unsheathed as good a sword
  As ever Saxon life-blood stained.
But vainly Beara's prince and he
  Might hope that struggle to prolong,—
No Spanish aid came o'er the sea,
    Their friends grew weak, their foemen
      strong;
The true men of the land were slain,
  Cabins as well as castles crushed,
And far o'er Munster, hill and plain,
  The very sounds of life were hushed.
No cattle lowed from bawn or keep,
  No farmer delved with spade or plough:
None cared to sow, for who might reap,
  Or see the harvest planted now?

So dire the wreck the Saxons made
  With gun and sword, and burning brand,
That troops unkept by foreign aid,
  Would famish in the wasted land.[20]
Sad was the scene to Donal's view,
  As from the Sheehy heights he gazed;
But midst the Ulster hills, he knew,
  His country's flag was still upraised.
O'Rourke, O'Cahan, brave O'Neill,
Despite the Saxons' gold and steel,
  Their treacherous arts, their subtle plans,
·Still filled the Pale with woe and dread,
Still on to battle bravely led
  The remnants of their broken clans.
'Twas now his sole remaining course
  On to their lands to travel fast;
To add to theirs his shattered force,
  And fight the good fight to the last.

———————

Fair Eileen, prized and treasured long
  All treasures of the Earth above,
Whose life was sweetened like a song,
  With tender thought and glowing love;
Whose lightest wish had power to sway
  Brave hearts that battle never shook,
Whom chiefs were happy to obey,
  Rewarded by one sunny look—

How sadly changed those hours that roll,
   While hid from war's destroying blast,
With nought to cheer her sorrowing soul,
   Her days and nights of gloom went past;
While Donal and his war-worn clan,
   On Muskerry's fields the fight maintained,
And but one trusty humble man
   To guard her and her babes remained —
Mac Sweeny — ever faithful found,
   Faithful of heart, and strong of arm,
Who midst wild dangers gathering round,
   Would shield his precious charge from harm.
Well did he guard the princely brood,
   Bantierna* and her darling sons,
He robbed the eaglets of their food
   To feed the young O'Sullivans,[21]
From the bright stream hooked up the trout,
   Trapped the fleet hare in copse and field,
And rude but bounteous fare spread out
   Where Donal's loves were safe concealed.
He sung old songs in accents low,
   To tunes the babes were pleased to hear,
He told strange tales of long ago,
   To charm awhile their mother's ear,
And held, like fosterer true and brave,
The trust his honoured master gave.

He came, the Prince of Beara came,
   To that dear nook within the glen,

   * *Bantierna*—The Lady of the land; the Chieftainess.

Toil-worn and vanquished, still the same
Unclouded brow, unbending frame,
   And eyes of sparkling light, as when
Around Dunboy his single name
   Could summon twice a thousand men.
The same to gentle Eileen too,
   As in those unforgotten days,
When from her fond young heart he drew
The glowing love that pure and true
   Still burned with calm and quenchless blaze.
He clasped her neck, he kissed her brow,
   He dried the tears she wept with joy,
And owned as deep a gladness now,
   As aught he felt in proud Dunboy.

He came—'twas come to this—to take,
For their dear lives, and honour's sake,
His loved ones thence ; to bear them forth
On that dread journey to the north,
For now by Beare or Bantry's shore
Who owned his blood was safe no more.
His faithful people, wild with grief,
Gathered around their glorious chief,
Men, women, children, all would go
Where'er he went—in weal or woe,
In war or peace, would share his lot,
But make no home where he was not.
He sent not from his exile band,
The slow of step. the weak of hand,

Who swelled the crowd, though well he knew
His danger with their number grew;
He placed the feebler forms within
A triple rank of sturdy men,
And all, one dark December day,
From Beara took their mournful way.

God help the weak! the world, alas!
Will use them hardly as they pass:
God pity Ireland! she has nurst
Of all her foes the fiercest, worst.
Her children's ablest plans were laid
That Irish blood might be betrayed,
Her warriors struck their hardest when
The blows fell on their countrymen,
And scarce one deed of guilt and shame
The strangers, from the day they came,
Wrought in the wronged and outraged land,
Unaided by a native hand.

Onward the sad procession sped,
   Fast fell the rain and winter snows,
The way was long, and rough to tread—
O bitter news, O tale of dread—
   Upon them pressed a cloud of foes!
The settlers of the English Pale,
Swept forth from every wooded vale,
And Irish traitors rushed before,
To dip their hands in Irish gore.

Dire was the hapless clansmen's flight,
They fought by day, they fought at night;[22]
Midst Muskery's hills they strove and bled,
Liscarroll's fields they streaked with red.
Base Barry, with his murderous brood,
And Teige Mac Carthy's men, pursued.
From rough Sliebh Lougher, Cuffey's troops,
Clan Gibbon's fierce and eager groups,
All hurried forward to destroy
The flying tribe from far Dunboy.
Well fought the clan, but field and flood,
The course they went was marked with blood,
And slain and famished bodies lay
Behind them on their fatal way.

They stood upon the Shannon's side,
The flood ran fast, the way was wide,
No ford was there to travel o'er,
No boats to bear them to the shore,
While nearer, like a rushing flame,
Tipperary's Saxon sheriff came.
Hard was their strait, at last bereft
Of every chance, what hope was left?
In gloom each head awhile was bowed,
Till spoke the Prince of Beare aloud—

" Let skiffs of osier twigs be made,
   Kill you your horses, let a hide
Tight on each wicker frame be laid,
   Launch the light curraghs on the tide,

Step softly in: what more to say
   To boatmen nursed on Bantry Bay?"

Soon on the waves the curraghs tossed,
From land to land they safely crossed,
But just as half the shattered ranks
Were landed on the further banks,
Upon the yet remaining few,
The sheriff's savage party flew.
Bloody and brief the fight that sped,
Ere back the beaten Palesmen fled,
And the light curraghs onward bore
The victors to the Galway shore.

One thousand persons, young and old,
   They marched from Bantry's deep blue tide,
Two hundred—every mortal told,
   They stood upon the Shannon's side,
And hardships worse than aught they met.
Lay in the path before them yet.
By Aughrim's slopes, beside a wood,
An English force well posted stood,
Trained soldiers all, and ably led,
With captain Malby at their head,
In numbers thrice exceeding those
Whose way they gathered to oppose,
And sworn to leave no living man
That evening of the rebel clan.

But on the desperate patriots dashed,
    Undaunted by that stern array,
Like tongues of fire their weapons flashed,
    As on they clove and dug their way
Through yielding ranks; like men possessed,
    They raged amidst the Saxon mass,
Strong men went down where'er they pressed,
    Like broken reeds or trampled grass.
On through the battle, to and fro,
    The Prince of Beara fiercely fought,
Who saw his restless eyes, might know
    That for some certain foe he sought.
One moment more, that foe was seen,
'Twas Malby—none might stand between
    The chieftains as with tiger bound
They leaped to meet, they fenced, they gripped,
Turned, twisted, straightened, sudden slipped,
    And rolled upon the bloody ground.
Turned o'er and o'er, with limbs inlocked,
Now struggling hard, now slowly rocked
With balanced strength: one moment grown
Stiff as one solid block of stone,
Next moment quick with vigorous life,
Two forms, but grasped in mortal strife.
Another pause, the longest since
The fight began;—uprose the Prince,
His red right hand held by the hair
    The English captain's severed head.
He flung the trophy high in air—
Burst from the Irish ranks a cheer—

Hurra, hurra! what troops could then
Withstand that rush of joyful men—
The Saxons wavered, shrunk with fear,
    Turned from the bloody field and fled.[23]

But, to the clansmen, dire the cost
Of every fight they won or lost.
From each attack they battled through,
Their dwindling force emerged more few,
And fainter, fewer, now they stood,
Than when they crossed the Shannon's flood.
Still onward pressed the warrior band,
Till on O'Rourke of Breifny's land,
Tired, wounded, faint, at length they found
One friendly spot of Irish ground.

Their rest was short, their stay was brief,
The brave O'Rourke, bowed down with grief,
Surrounded by the spreading Pale,
His wasted strength of no avail,
Foemen to check, or friends to save,
Submission to the Saxons gave.
But Beara's sons not even now
Beneath the hateful yoke would bow.
One chief still waged the patriot war,
And they would seek him, near or far.
Before their wounds had time to heal,
They bared again their glittering steel,
Went forth, and fought through conflicts stern.
Till by the brink of broad Lough Erne

The brave men stood—but thirty five
Out of one thousand left alive—
Then their's the woe, the grief to learn
In vain, in vain their long, long toil,
In vain their life-blood wet the soil,
He too surrendered—Hugh O'Neill!
And Ireland, like a swamp of gore,
Lay waste and still from shore to shore.

'Twas summer night, the rude winds slept,
As o'er the bay a vessel crept.
Two muffled forms went pacing slow
Along her smooth deck, to and fro,
Watching betimes the far stretched spars
Sway back and forward through the stars,
Pausing to hear the watch dogs' bark
From distant fields come through the dark,
And hear the heaving waters snore
Along the old familiar shore,
Whose headlands only met the sight
As gloomier patches of the night.
On passed the ship with easy glide,
Unto Bearehaven's tranquil tide;
Her low, black boat, in calm profound,
Bore on one form to Beara's ground.
He moved about with moody pace,
He travelled o'er and o'er the place,

8

Then, when the brightening of the day
Had warned him from the scene away,
He sought the sacred spot of all,
The ruin—once a castle tall—
And wept upon the broken wall.

On board! on board; fair blows the wind,
The Caha hills sink down behind;
Beare island dips, tall Hungry too,
Melts down into the sea of blue,
No more, except in dreams, to rise,
To Donal's or to Eileen's eyes.
Like winter rain, fast fell her tears,
And he, whose heart through troubled years
Its inward griefs in silence kept,
Bowed down his head, and wildly wept.

In Spain, high placed beside the king,
    The wearied exiles rest at last,
If honours, wealth, and peace could bring
    A charm to hide the painful past,
'Twas Donal's now;[21] but annals say
His heart was by his native bay;
His words were of the gallant men
Whose good swords flashed through pass and glen
Where'er he led; and when he thought
O'er all the wrongs the Saxon wrought,
The deep dyed crimes that Heaven must hate,
And God will punish, soon or late,

Oft did his thoughts break out aloud,
And many a time he firmly vowed
His race, though now proscribed and banned,
Would have and hold their native land,
And guard with patriot pride and joy,
The very stones of old Dunboy.

SONGS AND POEMS.*

FISHERMAN'S PRAYER.

The Sun is setting angrily,
  In threat'ning gusts the wind is blowing—
Holy Mary! Star of the Sea!
Speed our small bark fast and free
  O'er the homeward way we're going!

We left the land as the morning bright
  Purpled the smooth sea all before us—
We prayed to God, and our hearts were light,
We placed our bark in thy saving sight,
  And knew thou would'st well watch o'er us.

---

* The following pieces are re-printed from the *Nation* newspaper, to which journal they, with others not included in this volume, were contributed by the writer at various times within the past few years. Many of them received a large circulation from journals published in Ireland and in America—losing, in several cases, during their progress, the signature or initials attached to them on their first appearance, and acquiring new ones in place of them. Some "smart" gentleman, who gave his name, had one of them published in a Boston paper, with a line stating that he had written it expressly for that journal. They are indeed but small matters, yet the owner does not desire to see them appropriated by other persons; and, therefore, it is not unnecessary to preface their re-publication with this note.

But now the sun sets angrily,
    From black wild clouds the wind is blowing—
Holy Mary! Star of the Sea!
Send our small bark fast and free
    O'er the darkling way we're going!

We fished the deep the live-long day,
    The waves were rich, through God's good plea-
      sure;
We ventured far from our own bright bay,
And lingered late; we fain would stay
    'Till filled with the shining treasure.

But now the night falls threat'ningly,
    The sea runs high with the fierce wind blowing—
Holy Mary! Star of the Sea!
Our light, our guide, our safety be,
    O'er the stormy way we're going!

We pass the point where the tempest's strain
    Is lightened off by the land's high cover;
Our village lights shine out again—
I know my own in my window pane,
    And the tall church glooming over.

Holy Mary! Star of the Sea!
    With grateful love our hearts are glowing:
Behold we bless thy Son and thee!
Oh, still our light and safety be
    O'er the last dread course we're going!

A SOLDIER'S WAKE.

"A young soldier of the 18th Royal Irish, named Mac Donnell, was blown to atoms before Sebastopol. A few days since, our young hero's widowed mother had his medal with four clasps presented to her, the only relic of her son. In the course of the evening the poor woman 'laid out' the medal on the kitchen table, and having procured four mould candles, she collected her neighbours and kept up the 'wake' until an early hour the following morning.—*Tralee Paper.*

And this is all she has to lay
   To-night upon the snowy sheets
Before the friends who come the way,
   And sighing take their humble seats—
This medal, bravely, dearly won,
Poor token of her gallant son.

But over this, as nought beside
   Of him she loved to her remains,
The lights are lit, the croon is cried,
   And women weep in saddest strains,
While men who knew his boyhood well,
Say, foes went down before he fell.

These clasps and medal; only these!
   For this she nursed and loved him long,
She rocked him softly on her knees,
   And filled his ears with pleasant song,
And saw him, with a mother's pride,
Grow up and strengthen by her side.

Till bright with manhood's glowing charms
   He in his turn her nurse became,
He clasped her in his manly arms,
   And fondly propped her drooping frame.
Her step grew weak, her eye grew dim,
But then she lived and moved in him.

He went; he joined the deadly fight,
   His true heart loved her not the less;
But these are all she has to-night
   To light and cheer her loneliness,—
These silver honours, dearly won,
Poor tokens of her gallant son.

But even these, to-morrow morn,
   When lights burn out and friends depart,
Shall round her withered neck be worn,
   Shall lie upon her weary heart
Till death, for his dear memory's sake,
And then—shall deck another wake.

STEERING HOME.

Far out beyond our sheltered bay,
   Against the golden evening sky,
A brown speck rises, then away
   It sinks—it dwindles from my eye.

Again it rises; drawing nigh,
 Its well known shape grows sharp and clear—
 It is his bark, my Donal dear!
And oh! though small a speck it be,
 Kind Heaven, that knows my hope and fear,
Can tell the world it holds for me.

My boat of boats is steering home—
 She bends and sways before the wind;
I cannot see the milky foam
 Beneath her bows and far behind.
 ʿ But oh! I know my love will find,
 Howe'er the evening current flows,
 Howe'er the rising night wind blows,
The shortest course his keel can dart
 From where he is, to where he knows
I wait to clasp him to my heart.

Come, Donal, home! See by my side
 Your little sons, impatient too.
All day they loitered by the tide,
 And prattled of your boat and you.
 Into the glancing waves they threw
 Some little chips: the surges bore
 Their tiny vessels back to shore,
Then would they clap their hands and say
 The first was your's: then o'er and o'er,
Would ask me why you stayed away.

Come, Donal, home!   The red sun sets;
   Come to your children dear, and me;
And bring us full or empty nets,
   A scene of joy our hearth shall be.
You'll tell me stories of the sea;
   And I will sing the songs you said
Were sweet as wild sea-music made
By mermaids on the weedy rocks,
   When in some sheltered quiet shade,
They sing, and comb their dripping locks.

He comes! he comes!   My boat is near;
   I know her mainsail's narrow peak.
They haul her flowing sheets—I hear
   The dry sheeves on their pivots creak.
He waves his hand; I hear him speak—
   Come to the beach, my sons, with me;
He'll greet us from her side; and we
Shall meet him when he leaps to shore;
   Then take him home, and bid him see
Our brighter deck—our cottage floor.

—⚬—

TO MY BROTHER.

Though Fate will permit us no longer
   To struggle through life side by side,
Let our love but grow purer and stronger,
   However our hearts may be tried.

We are parted—it may be for ever—
  But, though we be far from each other,
One bond that no distance can sever
  Shall always connect us, my Brother.

And oft, when my prospects look dreary,
  When those I have trusted, deceive;
When I sink, disappointed and weary,
  And scarcely know what to believe;
When the dark clouds of life gather o'er me,
  One star shall outshine every other;
And the long, rugged pathway before me
  Grow bright with the love of my Brother.

How oft does some sweet recollection,
  From various occasions, arise,
That touches the chords of affection,
  And brings a hot dew to my eyes—
How oft does some incident waken
  The thoughts I could share with no other;
And my heart, like a chamber forsaken,
  Re-echo my wish for my Brother!

As barques that the tempests have driven
  And tossed far apart on the main,
Steer on by the beacons of Heaven,
  And meet in one harbour again;
Even so, if the storms of existence
  Have parted us here from each other,
Let us steer to that light in the distance,
  And meet in that haven, my Brother!

WESTWARD, HO!

My Mary ban,* 'tis nearly dawn,
   Come down, my Mary dear;
And let not those, our sleeping foes,
   Your passing footsteps hear.
For should they wake, my life they'd take,
   Or take away from me
My more than life, my plighted wife—
   My Mary ban, machree.

My love, my pride, the world is wide,
   And wheresoe'er we roam,
We've strength, and youth, and love, and truth,
   To build ourselves a home.
There's nought but care and sorrow here
   In everything I see;
And nothing bright, by day or night,
   But Mary ban, machree.

My love! I knew your word was true;
   Your heart was strong and brave.
We'll seek, asthore, the better shore
   That smiles beyond the wave!

---

* ban—pronounced "bawn", means fair.

Our lot, we know, where'er we go,
 A lot of toil must be ;
But yet away we start to-day,
 My Mary ban, machree.

—◦◦—

A SERENADE.

———--

My Lady fair ! thy gentle slumbers
 Will not shut out this lay of mine,
But through thine ear its plaintive numbers
 Shall steal into thy dreams divine.
The murmur of a streamlet flowing
 Through sunny lands, the strain may be,
Or wind through blossomed foliage blowing,
 But yet 'twill breathe of love and thee.

And when from thy bright dreams awaking,
 Those plaintive notes thou still shalt hear,
Upon the night wind softly breaking,
 While all beside is dark and drear ;
Then fancy's wiles no more misleading,
 Thy heart will know the strain to be
The fond appeal, the fervent pleading,
 That bursts from mine for love and thee.

Like some pale plant in darkness pining,
  That struggles toward the one bright **ray**
Into its cheerless prison shining,
  So I too fade and pine away ;
And so I creep unto thy dwelling,
  Before thy window pane, to see
The light that, gloom and grief dispelling,
  Falls on my soul from love and thee.

The path I've traced is dark and lonely,
  And distant far my cottage lies,
But let me hear thy voice, and only
  One moment see thy beaming eyes!
Then dangers wild may wait before me—
  Then Heaven may hide its stars from me,
And thunders burst around and o'er me,
  I'll only think of love and thee.

—⊃⊂—

THE LITTLE WIFE.

Frown not, my love! ah, let me chase
  Away the shade of care that lies
To-night so darkly on your face,
  And mist-like o'er your manly eyes.
Ah, let me try the winning ways

You said were mine—the angel art
To pour at once ten thousand rays
  Of dancing sunlight on your heart!
      My love, my life!
      Your little wife
Must bid these gloomy thoughts depart.

When love was young and hopes were bright,
  I thought, 'midst all our dreams of bliss,
That clouds might come like these to-night,
  And hours of sorrow such as this.
And then, I said, my task shall be
  To soothe his heart so fond and true,
And he who loves me thus, shall see
  How much his little wife can do.
      My heart, my life,
      Your little wife
Must bid you dream those dreams anew.

Then let me lift those locks that fall
  So wildly o'er your lofty brow,
And smooth, with fingers soft and small,
  The veins that cord your temples now.
How oft, when ached your wearied head,
  From manly care, or thought divine,
You've held me to your heart, and said
  You wanted love so deep as mine!
      My own, my life!
      Your little wife,
That love is all her life's design.

And here it is—a love as wild
　　As e'er defied the world's control;
The fondness of a tearful child,
　　The passion of a woman's soul,
All mingled in my breast for thee,
　　In one hot tide—I cannot speak:
But feel my throbbing heart, and see
　　Its brightness in my burning cheek—
　　　　My love, my life!
　　　　Your little wife
　　Must cheer you, or her heart will break.

Ah, now the breast I found so cold,
　　Grows warm within my close embrace;
And smiles as sweet as those of old
　　Are stealing softly o'er your face;
And far within your brightening eyes
　　My image, true and clear, I see;
Each shade of care and sorrow flies,
　　And leaves your heart again to me—
　　　　My love, my life!
　　　　Your little wife
　　Its only Queen must ever be.

—◦◦—

A WINTER NIGHT.

Come on, come on, my heart of hearts,
    Come fondly nigh to me :
Our hearth is bright this wintry night,
    Howe'er the skies may be.
Dark clouds have cloaked our darling moon,
    There's not a star to see ;
My moon, my star, my sun you are,
    And more than all to me.

To-night the wind is howling loud
    Through turrets grand and high ;
With softer rush, with swell and hush,
    We hear it hurry by.
The rain upon our cottage thatch
    Is drifting noiselessly—
So soft may all life's tempests fall
    On you, my love, and me.

Or let them bring us icy words,
    And looks as cold as snow—
They'll melt before our cottage door,
    We'll thaw them where we go.
They cannot touch our hearts of fire,
    Or dim those eyes of blue,
Or e'er unfold the clasp I hold,
    My heart of hearts, of you.

Or let the winter last for aye,
　　Let all its rain be hail,
Let clouds the worst around us burst,
　　And wild words load the gale.
I still shall have a summer bright,
　　A flower of fairest hue,
And light and heat, and fruitage sweet,
　　My heart of hearts, in you.

— ⚬ —

THE LITTLE BARQUE.

Oh! sailor from yon stately ship,
　　Whose wet sails tell a stormy tale,
Tell me if on your fearful trip
You've seen a small barque roll and dip,
　　And live throughout the gale?

She left these shores when winds were low,
　　With white sails set and flag unfurled;
Her crew were told those gales would blow,
Those thunders burst—yet would they go,
　　And brave the stormy world.

" I've passed the barque far out at sea,
　　Along the mountain waves she flew;
The waters boiled beneath her lee,
Her spars were bent as spars could be,
　　Yet fearless seemed the crew.

"And like a bird she swept along,
　　With white sails set, and flag unfurled;
The storm around was mixed with song,
She gilt the waves she rolled among,
　　And proudly braved the world.

"And ever upward looked the crew,
　　As if to say, ' though dark it be,
The brilliant sun will yet burst through,
Light clouds will fleck a sky of blue,
　　And soft winds sweep the sea'.

"She passed ; she faded from my sight,
　　The darkness fell.　I only say,
That barque whose freight was love and
　　light,
Might weather through so wild a night,
　　When passed was such a day".

God bless the barque and bless the crew,
　　And as they hope, so may it be,
That brilliant suns will soon burst through,
Light clouds soon fleck a sky of blue,
　　And soft winds sweep the sea.

— ✤ —

HOME! HOME!

In great Columbia's grandest town,
   I toil and think the whole day long;
And sometimes sigh, but never frown,
   For Hope still sings a cheerful song—
     " Toil, toil away,
      Fast comes the day,
        When once again your eyes shall see
      Your own dear isle,
      And her whose smile
        Is dearer still to thee".

Lean o'er your anchor, Hope divine,
   I inly cry; oh, tell me more
Of her whose pure young heart was mine,
   And yet may be, this trial o'er.
     " Her large white brow
      Is calmer now—
        More woman sweet her face appears;
      Her brown eyes seem
      For aye to dream,
        And not unused to tears".

Again I bend me o'er my task,
   With nerves new strung and gladdened will;
Yet something more my heart would ask;
   A shadow haunts my spirit still—

Her love? Her truth?
Her vows of youth?
   "She steals away with face all pale,
To gaze each day
O'er ocean's spray,
   For some expected sail".

Kind Hope! oh! bid her not to fear
  My heart is changed, or vows were vain.
I will not linger longer here,
  But haste across the stormy main
    That rolls and raves
    In mountain waves,
     Between my native land and me—
    My own dear isle,
    And her whose smile
     I've pined so long to see.

And with the wealth my hands have won,
  One home shall soon be hers and mine,
A cottage fronting to the sun,
  A few bright fields, and glossy kine;
    And we shall tread
    The soil, nor dread
     The village tyrant as of yore,
    But sow and reap,
    And wake and sleep,
     Secure for evermore.

SONG FROM THE BACKWOODS.

Deep in Canadian woods we've met,
  From one bright island flown ;
Great is the land we tread, but yet
  Our hearts are with our own.
And ere we leave this shanty small,
  While fades the autumn day,
    We'll toast old Ireland !
    Dear Old Ireland !
    Ireland, boys, Hurra !

We've heard her faults a hundred times,
  The new ones and the old,
In songs and sermons, rants and rhymes,
  Enlarged some fifty fold.
But take them all, the great and small,
  And this we've got to say :—
    Here's dear old Ireland !
    Good Old Ireland !
    Ireland, boys, Hurra !

We know that brave and good men tried
  To snap her rusty chain,
That patriots suffered, martyrs died,
  And all, 'tis said, in vain ;
But no, boys, no ! a glance will show

How far they've won their way—
    Here's good Old Ireland!
    Loved Old Ireland!
    Ireland, boys, Hurra!

We've seen the wedding and the wake,
    The patron and the fair;
The stuff they take, the fun they make,
    And the heads they break down there,
With a loud "hurroo" and a "pillalu",
    And a thundering "clear the way!"—
    Here's gay Old Ireland!
    Dear Old Ireland!
    Ireland, boys, Hurra!

And well we know in the cool gray eves,
    When the hard day's work is o'er,
How soft and sweet are the words that greet
    The friends who meet once more;
With "Mary machree!" and "My Pat! 'tis he!'
    And "My own heart night and day!"
    Ah, fond old Ireland!
    Dear Old Ireland!
    Ireland, boys, Hurra!

And happy and bright are the groups that pass
    From their peaceful homes, for miles
O'er fields, and roads, and hills, to Mass,
    When Sunday morning smiles!

And deep the zeal their true hearts feel
  When low they kneel and pray.
    Oh, dear old Ireland!
    Blest Old Ireland!
    Ireland, boys, Hurra!

But deep in Canadian woods we've met,
  And we never may see again
The dear old isle where our hearts are set,
  And our first fond hopes remain!
But come, fill up another cup,
  And with every sup let's say—
    Here's loved old Ireland!
    Good Old Ireland!
    Ireland, boys, Hurra!

—∘c—

THE IRISH-AMERICAN.

Columbia the free is the land of my birth,
And my paths have been all on American earth;
But my blood is as Irish as any can be,
And my heart is with Erin afar o'er the sea.

My father, and mother, and friends all around,
Are daughters and sons of the sainted old ground—
They rambled its bright plains and mountains
    among,
And filled its fair valleys with laugh and with song.

But I sing their sweet music, and often they own
It is true to old Ireland in style and in tone;
I dance their gay dances, and hear them with glee
Say each touch tells of Erin afar o'er the sea.

I have tufts of green shamrock in sods they
    brought o'er,
I have shells they picked up ere they step; ed
    from the shore,
I have books that are treasures; the fondest
    I hold
Is "The Melodies", clasped and nigh covered
    with gold.

My pictures are pictures of scenes that are dear,
For the beauties they are, or the glories they
    were,
And of good men and great men whose merits
    shall be
Long the pride of green Erin afar o'er the sea.

If I were in beautiful Dublin to-day,
To the spots I hold sacred I'd soon find my way,
For I know where O'Connell and Curran are laid,
And where loved Robert Emmett sleeps cold
    "in the shade".

And if I were in Wexford—how fondly I'd trace
Each field I have marked on my maps of the place,

9

Where the brave Ninety-Eight men poured hotly
    and free
Their blood for dear Erin afar o'er the sea.

Dear home of my fathers! I'd hold thee to blame,
And my cheeks would at times take the crimson
    of shame,
Did thy sad tale not show, in each sorrow-stained
    line,
That the might of thy tyrant was greater than
    thine.

But her soldiers are many, abroad and at home,
Her ships on all oceans are ploughing the foam,
And her wealth is untold—sure no equal was she
For poor plundered Erin afar o'er the sea.

Yet they tell me the strife is not yet given o'er—
That the gallant old Island will try it once more;
And will call, with her harp when her flag is
    unfurled,
Her sons, and *their* sons, from the ends of the
    world.

If so, I've a rifle that's true to a hair,
A brain that can plan and a hand that can dare;
And the summons will scarce have died out, when
    I'll be,
Mid the green fields of Erin afar o'er the sea.

FAR AWAY.

Far far away from my native land,
With a heavy heart and a weary hand,
My life is wasted in care and toil,
And my bones shall lie in a foreign soil.

I little thought that a few short years
Would quench my bliss in a tide of tears,
And see me fly o'er the ocean foam,
Like a lonely bird from a ruined home.

The grass grows high on my cottage floor,
The wild wind sighs through the open door;
The rain falls down, and the sunbeams shine,
Through the roof that once sheltered me and mine.

Still and cold is the hearth to-night,
Where the song was loud, and the laugh was light,
Where the neighbours came from their homes
    around,
And a loving welcome was always found.

Where the wife of my heart would sing to me
The Irish music that seemed to be
Some spirit's sighing, softly driven
Through the golden bars of the gates of Heaven.

But blight and ruin came down ere long,
And quelled the laughter and hushed the song;
And in the hour of our deep distress
The landlord's bosom was merciless.

And we were thrown on the roadside bare,
Where my darlings pined in the piercing air—
To my helpless form for awhile they clung,
But she was weak, and my boys were young.

I would I were in that soft green shade,
Where the grave of all that I loved I made,
To end my days, and to ease my woes,
By my dear ones' side in a long repose.

But, alas! far, far from my native land,
With a heavy heart and a weary hand,
My life is wasted in care and toil,
And my bones shall lie in a foreign soil.

—◦•—

THE OLD EXILE.

A youth to manhood growing,
With dark brown curls flowing,
O'er brow and temples glowing,
        I came across the sea;
And now my head is hoary,

But, land of song and story,
Green isle of ancient glory,
  My heart is still with thee.

Thy hopes still clung around me,
Thy bonds for ever bound me,
And all occasions found me
    Within the midst of those
Whose love was ever paid thee,
Who met to cheer and aid thee,
And at a distance made thee
    A terror to thy foes.

Long through this sad sojourning,
My heart and brain were burning
With hopes of yet returning
    To Erin glad and free;
My hopes were unavailing,
I feel my strength is failing,
And still that bitter wailing
    Is drifting o'er the sea.

But I have yet, thank Heaven,
Four gallant sons, of seven
My Irish wife has given,
    To soothe my heart's decline;
Four youths of noble bearing,
Of spirits high and daring,
Whose hearts are ever sharing
    Those cherished dreams of mine.

And should my dear land ever
Renew the old endeavour
Her fatal bonds to sever,
    Though I can strive no more,
Four soldiers brave I'll send her,
To aid her and defend her,
And thus I still can render
    Allegiance, as of yore.

I have one gentle daughter:
How fondly have I taught her
Of Erin o'er the water,
    An island green and fair;
And marked her bright eyes shining
As on my knees reclining,
I kissed her, while entwining
    Bright shamrocks in her hair.

Her mother's songs she sings me,
Sweet thoughts of home she brings me;
The secret pang that wrings me,
    Her breast can never know.
But Irish love so purely,
Runs through, I rest securely
Thereon, and say that surely,
    'Twill never nurse a foe.

But life is fading slowly,
My friends must lay me lowly
Far from that abbey holy

I loved through all the past.
The world grows dim before me
A broad wing closes o'er me—
But, Erin dear that bore me,
I love thee to the last.

—◦◦—

THE GREEN FLAG.

Let sages frown, let cynics sneer,
Let heartless cowards doubt and fear,
- Let traitors barter and betray,
And hollow friends go creep away ;
Through sun and shade, through good and ill,
We'll keep the Green Flag flying still,
Till o'er the isle, at length, we see
Its bright folds wave triumphantly !

Our band though small, our blades though few,
Have met the worst our foe can do ;
And if our cause could fail, we know
This strife had ended long ago ;
But now, by all that cause has cost,
Our sacred hope shall not be lost,
Above this isle we yet shall see
The Green Flag wave triumphantly !

The axe, the gibbet, and the chain,
Have done, and do their work in vain ;

Our martyrs fall, our heroes bleed,
But gallant men again succeed;
And, by the ashes of the dead,
The tears they wept, the blood they shed,
Above this isle we yet shall see
The Green Flag wave triumphantly!

—&—

MICHAEL DWYER.

———

"At length, brave Michael Dwyer, you and your
    trusty men
Are hunted o'er the mountains and tracked into
    the glen.
Sleep not, but watch and listen; keep ready
    blade and ball;
The soldiers know your hiding to-night in wild
    Emall".*

---

* The glen of Emall, in the county of Wicklow. For
a sketch of the adventures of Michael Dwyer, see Dr.
Madden's Lives of the United Irishmen. Many were
Dwyer's hair-breadth escapes, for some of which he was
indebted to the kindness of a soldier who used to give
him timely warning when the military were on his
track.

The soldiers searched the valley, and towards the
    dawn of day
Discovered where the outlaws, the dauntless
    rebels, lay
Around the little cottage they form'd into a ring,
And called out, "Michael Dwyer! surrender to
    the king!"

Thus answered Michael Dwyer: "Into this house
    we came,
Unasked by those who own it—they cannot be
    to blame.
Then let those peaceful people unquestioned pass
    you through,
And when they're placed in safety, I'll tell you
    what we'll do".

'Twas done; "And now", said Dwyer, "your
    work you may begin,
You are a hundred outside — we're only four
    within;
We've heard your haughty summons, and this
    is our reply.
We're true United Irishmen, we'll fight until we
    die".

Then burst the war's red lightning, then poured
    the leaden rain,
The hills around reëcho'd the thunder peals again.

The soldiers falling round him, brave Dwyer
    sees with pride,
But, ah! one gallant comrade is wounded by his
    side.

Yet there are three remaining, good battle still
    to do,
Their hands are strong and steady, their aim is
    quick and true—
But hark that furious shouting the savage sol-
    diers raise!
The house is fired around them! The roof is in
    a blaze!

And brighter every moment the lurid flame arose,
And louder swelled the laughter and cheering of
    their foes.
Then spake the brave M'Alister, the weak and
    wounded man,
"You can escape, my comrades, and this shall
    be your plan:

"Place in my hands a musket, then lie upon the
    floor,
I'll stand before the soldiers, and open wide the
    door,
They'll pour into my bosom the fire of their
    array;
Then, whilst their guns are empty, dash through
    them and away!"

He stood before his foemen, revealed amidst the
flame,
From out their levelled pieces the wished for
volley came.
Up sprang the three survivors for whom the
hero died,
But only Michael Dwyer burst through the ranks
outside.

He baffled his pursuers, who followed like the
wind;
He swam the river Slaney, and left them far
behind;
But many an English soldier he promised soon
should fall,
For these his gallant comrades who died in wild
Emall.

—◦○—

THEOBALD WOLFE TONE.

Brave heart, bold heart, and active brain,
What hopes and griefs were like to thine,
Thou patient worker, whose design
Was wrought till promised triumph shone
Upon its summit—then again
Was dashed to ruin—
Gallant Tone.

I see thy calm pure spirit rise
    Like some pale moon that takes its way
    Through storms that gathered all the day,
Yet looks when clouds apart have blown
As high and holy in the skies
    And bright as ever—
                Faithful Tone.

The force of earnest will, allied
    To fixéd purpose, and a mind
    Within whose crystal depths enshrined
The patriot's passion glowed alone,
Or fed on all that lived beside,
    Made up thy being—
                Fearless Tone.

Thine was the joy to win the ear
    And strong heart of a mighty land,
    To see her stretch an armed hand
With aid and cheering towards thine own,
To see the tyrant pale with fear,
    And Erin hopeful—
                Gallant Tone.

And thine the nameless grief to see
    The vision fade—the wild night fall,
    The storm burst fiercely forth, and all
Thy life-long labour overthrown,
The worst itself no worse could be
    To thy proud spirit—
                Hapless Tone.

PERTURBATIONS.

A certain planet in the sky,
   The star-seers often had perceived
Was much perturbed, they knew not why,
   'Twas their mistake, they first believed.
They blamed their glasses, blamed the way
   They'd taken down their observations,
And almost all agreed to say
   The fault was in their calculations.

But one, the keen Le Verrier, thought
   It was a fact, and had a cause
That might be found, if calmly sought,
   In nature's grand, eternal laws;
He said the orb inclined and swayed
   To some unknown, but strong attraction;
And, by a cool synthesis, made
   A cause to suit it to a fraction.

He said, there is—there must have been—
   Another planet circling near;
A planet I have never seen,
   But I'll engage the thing is there.
'Tis such a weight, and such a size,
   In such a line, at such a distance,
Whoever seeks as I advise,
   Will soon perceive its bright existence.

10

He wrote to Berlin to a man
   Whose fame was known the earth around,
And showed by logic, map, and plan,
   Where this new world should then be found.
The learned German turned his glass
   Upon the space so clearly given,
And soon the orb was seen to pass
   Amid the shining hosts of heaven.

A curious tale, and true beside;
   But here, as well as up on high,
I think the rule may be applied
   To finding more than meets the eye.
There's my friend Ned—I made, one night,
   A few such simple observations,
And soon found out the body bright
   That causes all his perturbations.

There's witty, gay, and pretty John,
   I've also found the hidden force
That sways his path, and draws him on
   In such a wild, eccentric course.
Poor Dick! his centripetal strength
   Was never great. One day we missed him,
And on Le Verrier's plan, at length,
   I've found him in another system.

In short I find in every case,
   The Frenchman's reasoning just and true,

Not only in the fields of space,
   But on our dusty planet too.
And when I see a strange effect,
   However long and well I've conned it,
I'll always strive to recollect,
   How bright a cause may lie beyond it.

—⁐c—

A VALENTINE

There's not a print-shop window in the city
   Without its stock of " valentines" displayed ;
All sorts and sizes.   Some are rather witty,
   And others scarcely civil, I'm afraid.
Each with a verse of some appropriate ditty,
   To suit the kind or cruel man or maid;
And some are frightful—sure such horrid features
Were never seen on any human creatures.

First, here's the genus " Swell"—a class of thing
   I have not found in Buffon or Linnæus.
The waist of each would fit into a ring ;
   The head of each, perhaps, holds three ideas.
With pretty lisp each seems to say or sing—
   " I wonder, demme, do the girls see us !
We surely must look stunnin now, good gracious,
With these cigars stuck deep in our moustachios".

Next comes that perfect beauty, young Miss
    Skinny,
Bedizened in the highest style of art;
Indeed a man would think it quite a sin he
    Should ever spoil her dress against his heart.
Dear tender soul, who dotes upon Bellini,
    And boasts no small acquaintance with Mozart—
In short, who lives in one perpetual jingle
Of "Take this ring", "All's lost", and "Do not
    "mingle".

And here are sylvan landscapes—woods and
    bowers,
    With pretty nooks wherein to sigh or swear,
And breechless Cupids roving through the flowers,
    The rosy urchins seeming not to fear
The bitter winds and long-continued showers
    Of this inclement season of the year,
But playing off their pranks and evolutions,
Regardless of their little constitutions.

Then here are buildings they've contrived so neatly,
    The doors and windows can be opened wide,
And at a single glance you see completely
    Whatever may be going on inside.
Perhaps the question has been murmured sweetly,
    Perhaps the lady's fainted and replied—
Or it may be, Papa in sobs addressing
The happy youth, saying "Take her, with my
    blessing".

Behold a church—the holy knot is tying
 Within its walls as tight as tight can be ;
And here's a cottage—turtle doves are flying
 About the roof and on from tree to tree ;
The very flowers upon the wall seem trying
 The precious thing within the room to see.
You look, and find (a slight anticipation)
A pretty, plump young " lord of the creation".

But none of these will suit me, and I fear
 My love must do without a valentine ;
.But stop an instant—yes, go bring me here
 That box of colours and those sheets of mine ;
I feel an artist's impulse——I declare
 I'll execute my own sublime design—
Oh ! honoured ghosts of all the great Italians,
Now crowd around me in your bright battalions !

Inspire my heart and guide my daring hand,
 Raffaelle, Buonarotti, Cimabue !
Give me a little of your old command
 O'er all the lights and shades of every hue.
Oh, bear my soul away to Fancy-land—
 But bring it back—be very sure you do,
For some one here—nor do I mean to doubt it—
Declares, indeed, she could not do without it.

Dear little maiden, vain is all endeavour
 To paint the love my heart would send to thee.

I'll only say, that heart is thine for ever,
   That love is deep as human love can be.
I'll only tell thee, pen or pencil never
   Drew form so fair and dear as thine to me,
And these fond truths, I know, will please thee
      better
Than smart quotations or a pictured letter.

—⁕—

MY POETESS.

When I was young and sentimental,
   And my head was, day and night,
Filled with fancies transcendental,
   Dazzled with the Poet's light,
Well, said I, I'll love for ever,
   But I'll never wed, unless
I shall meet some very clever,
   Gentle, thoughtful, Poetess.

In the course of my researches,
   I confess I met a few
Boasting of some household virtues,
   Let me see!—some one or two
Knew the current price of mutton,
   Some could make a paste or pie,
Others sew a loosened button—
   Not the thing for me, said I.

Yet I never minded sobbing,
   For, like Lamartine, I knew
That a heart was somewhere throbbing
   To my own with pulses true;
But the thing was how to get it,
   Long I thought, but could not guess,
And I own I somewhat fretted
   For my gentle Poetess.

But I found her; oh, I found her!
   'Tis no matter where or how,
Such a brightness all around her!
   Such a light upon her brow!
Ask not sate she at a window
   With a sampler or a book,
Did I take her for Belinda,
   Or the ghost of Lalla Rookh.

Ask not did I woo her kneeling,
   Did I rather choose to stand—
Did I pour a flood of feeling
   In the style of Madame Sand;
Heed not had she much of Norah
   Creina in her silken dress,
Or the visage of Medora;
   But I found my Poetess.

Ah! the vulgar way of doing
   Such a work as ours that night—

Oh, the joy, the bliss of wooing
    At a true poetic height!
Bright ideas interchanging,
    Wingéd fancies flitting by,
Glorious thoughts for ever ranging
    From our planet to the sky!

Thrillings, throbbings, sweet sensations,
    Airy strains divinely mixed—
Halos, flashes, scintillations,
    Suns and systems, loose and fixed,
Floated round us, seemed to pass us,
    Oh, the nameless happiness
Of making love on Mount Parnassus
    To a gentle Poetess!

Yet at times through all my pleasure
    Ran a vague mysterious fear,
Lest the Gods should see my treasure,
    Lest some spirit hovering near
With more than human passion burning,
    Should take her off, his home to bless,
And leave me musically mourning
    For my gentle Poetess.

But they well declined committing
    Such a grievous piece of wrong,
And I won her in befitting
    Snatches of extatic song.

Those who doubt or question whether
    I was wise, or acted well,
Let them come along together
    To the cottage where we dwell.

Enter here—no power refuses
    Though he come from halls above;
'Tis the temple of the Muses
    And the sweet abode of Love.
Never heed the small confusion,
    Who could well expect it less,
In the dignified seclusion
    Of a gifted Poetess?

Playing with the fender irons,
    Scratching at each other's eyes,
See the little Moores and Byrons,
    Hear their laughter and their cries!
See them cut their little capers
    Till they get some rapid smacks,
For disturbing all the papers,
    On their faces, or their backs.

Hear Letitia Hemans Browning
    Loudly squalling to be fed,
See young Scott take like a drowning
    Hold of cross Childe Harold's head.
You can't see our little Dryden,
    Being gone to sleep, I guess,

He's the one I ought to pride in,
　Says my gentle Poetess.

Shelly is to get a powder,
　He's not well, I grieve to say,
And his cries, though there are louder,
　Pierce me in a dreadful way.
Little Pope, I fear, will never
　Very tall or healthy be,
Meeting accidents for ever,
　Most unfortunate is he.

Then of course we've nymphs attendant,
　Luna seeks in spite of fate
To keep the fender quite resplendant,
　And raise a polish on the grate.
There you see our blooming Hebé,
　Unto whose especial care
We confide our precious baby,
　Paying two pounds ten a year.

Then there's Mercury, her first cousin,
　And Egeria, of the springs,
Who does our washing by the dozen,
　And never counts the baby things.
There are also other graces,
　I must say a loving three,
But they've advertised for "places",
　And they'll soon be leaving me.

Well, howe'er the world may view it,
    Call it trouble, tumult, noise,
I am quite accustomed to it,
    And I love my girls and boys.
Should a youth to-day come seeking
    Hints from me on happiness,
I should tell him, plainly speaking,
    Win a gentle Poetess.

—◦◦—

NOTES TO DUNBOY.

"Shoots of the grand old Spanish vine".

In a letter of Donal O'Sullivan to the King of Spain, which is printed in the *Pacata Hibernia* (an authentic account of the wars of Queen Elizabeth in Ireland, compiled by Sir George Carew, Lord President of Munster, afterwards Earl of Totness, who was one of the chief actors in those wars), the following passage occurs :—

" We the meere Irish long sithence deriving our roote and originall from the famous and most noble race of the Spaniards: viz., from Milecius, sonne to Bile, sonne to Breogwin, and from Lwighe, sonne to Lythy, sonne to Breogwin, by the testimony of our old ancient bookes of antiquities, our Petigrees, our Histories, and our Cronicles. Though there were no other matter, wee came not as naturall branches of the famous tree, whereof we grew, but beare a hearty loue, and naturall affection, and intire inclination of our hearts and minds to our ancient most loving kingsfolkes, and the most noble race whereof we descended".

This Breogwin, grandfather to Milesius, was one of the Kings of Spain. About 1,000 years before the Christian era the three sons of Milesius led an expedition into Ireland. The names of the three brothers were Heber, Heremon, and Ir. They divided the country between them. Heremon had Leinster and Connaught; Ir had Ulster; Heber had Munster. In the second century of the Christian era, Eogan More, King of Munster, one of the descendants of the Heber above mentioned, was married to the Spanish Princess Beara, daughter to Heber, King of Castile. By this marriage Eogan More had a son, Oilioll Olum, who became King of Munster. Oilioll had three sons—Eogan, Cormac Cas, and Kian.

From Kian were descended the clan Kian; from Cormac Cas, the Daleassians; from Eogan, the Eugenians. The O'Sullivans are of the Eugenian line, and took their name from Suileabhan, one of their chiefs, in the tenth century.—*From the notes to Connellan's Edition of the Four Masters.*

Note 2, Page 10.

" And cheered with like rewards their work
Who fight the Saxon and the Turk".

Pope Gregory XIII. (A.D. 1580) granted to all who should fight against the English in Ireland an indulgence, of which he said—" This is the same indulgence as that which was imparted to those who fought against the Turks for the recovery of the Holy Land". Some years subsequently (A D. 1600) Pope Clement VIII. sent similar indulgences to Ireland, and sent a present of a plume of phœnix feathers to Hugh O'Neill, the leader of the patriot forces. Judging from the religious and reverential character of Donal O'Sullivan, as revealed in his letters, those facts must have powerfully influenced him in his opposition to the English power in Ireland.

Note 3, Page 10.

" What though in London's gloomy tower
Desmond and brave MacCarthy pine".

" The Catholic cause suffered considerably at this time by the arrest of James, son of Thomas Fitzgerald, commonly called Earl of Desmond, and Florence MacCarthy, of the illustrious house of Mac Carthy Riagh, who had married the daughter and heiress of Mac-Carthy More, Baron of Valentia, and Earl of Clancar".—*MacGeoghegan's History of Ireland.* The *Pacata* contains a curious history of the " Juggling" of this Florence MacCarthy. He certainly appears to have played fast and loose with both parties, but the cause to which he was really attached was that of his country; and of all men Carew ought to be the last to complain indignantly of a little "juggling".

For a full account of the above-mentioned and the other Earls of Desmond, see the History of the Geraldines. by Brother Dominicus O'Daly, a translation of which, by the Rev. C. P. Meehan, has been published by James Duffy.

Note 4, Page 10.

" We spurn her peace, we cast away
Her patent for our fathers' lands".

" In the twelfth year of the reign of Queen Elizabeth, Sir Owen O'Sullivan, in order to establish a substantial title to the countries he then held, surrendered them to the Queen, and received a formal grant thereof by patent. This measure gave rise to a long suit at law between Sir Owen and his nephew Donal McDonal O'Sullivan, the latter of whom endeavoured to prove that his uncle had usurped the possession at the death of his (Donal's) father. The suit terminated by a letter of partition, dated January, 1593, under the Great Seal, being issued to plot out the lands and castles of Bere, Bantry, Ardea, and others belonging to the O'Sullivans. The castles and dependencies of Bere were alotted to Donal, and Bantry, etc., to Sir Owen".— *Wild's Killarney.*

Note 5, Page 19.

" Sword and spear
They stuck into the ground upright,
And blest with many a form and prayer".

That this manner of blessing their arms was a custom of the Irish in those and in earlier days, is stated by one of the Anglo-Irish chroniclers.

Note 6, Page 24.

" First of the ranks still firm and true
Were Donal's, Beara's gallant few".

O'Sullivan's little force was amongst those who made the most determined fight on the disastrous day of Kinsale, and when the battle was lost, it bravely protected some of the retreating troops of the northern chieftains, who but for such protection would have suffered more severely than they did.

Note 7, Page 24.

" 'Twas long foretold, the wise men say".

Carew, in the *Pacata Hibernia*, having given an account of the defeat of the Irish and Spaniards at Kinsale, says:—" Although no man is lesse credulous than myselfe is of idle prophesies, the most whereof are coyned after things are done, yet I make bold to relate this which succeeds, for long time before the thing I speake of was brought to light: myselfe was an eye-witnesse when it was reported; in concealing it I should wrong the trueth, which makes mee bold to remember it. Many times I did heare the Earle of Thomond tell the Lord President that in an old booke of Irish prophesies which hee had scene, it was reported that towards the latter dayes there should bee a battell fought betweene the English and tho Irish in a place which the booke nameth, neere unto Kinsale. The Earle of Thomond comming out of England, and landing first at Castlehaven, and after at Kinsale, as aforesaid: in the time of the siege myselfe and divers others heard him again report the prophesie to the President, and named the place where (according to the prophesie) the field should bee fought. The day whereupon the victorie was obtained, the Lord President and the Earle rode out to see the dead bodies of the vanquished, and the President asked some that were there present by what name that ground was called; they not knowing to what end hee did demand it, told him the true name thereof, which was the same which the Earle so often before had reported to the President. I beseech the reader to belieue mee, for I deliver nothing but trueth: but as one swallow makes no summer, so shall not this one true prophesie increase my credulitie in old predictions of that kinde".

Note 8, Page 32.

" No plot is spurned, no bribe is spared,
   No dark device of traitor art".

Carew, as we learn from his own account of himself, was a consummate rogue. In his work, the *Pacata Hibernia*, he has given us many specimens of his subtlety and dishonesty. When he had arrived at Bantry, on his way to besiege Dunboy, he wrote a letter to the Spanish gunners who remained with O'Sullivan, informing them that if, when the English forces were in front of the castle, they would leave it and come to his camp, he would have them passed safely into Spain. "This above written", said he, "I am obliged by my promise to Don Juan to fulfil. But if you haue a desire to finde or reciue further favours at my hands, you may with facilitie deserue it, that is, when you leaue the castle to cloy the Ordnance, or mayme their Carriages, that when they shall haue need of them they may prooue uselesse, for the which I will forthwith liberally recompense you answerable to the qualitie of your merit". The Spaniards despised the traitorous proposition, and fought their guns to the last. Again it is clear from the terms in which the affair is spoken of in the *Pacata*, and from the character of Carew, that in the interview held a few days previous to the siege with Richard MacGeohegan 'on Bere Island, an endeavour was made to seduce that brave and faithful chieftain from the service of O'Sullivan. But in this case, as in that of the Spaniards, the effort proved of no avail. After the capitulation at Kinsale, while Don Juan, who had commanded the Spanish forces there, was on the most friendly terms with him, Carew exercised his talents by practising on the Spaniard a gross deception and violation of faith. A messenger having arrived from Spain with some letters from the King and others, and "the Lord Deputies (Mountjoy's) heart itching to have the letters in his hands, he prayed the President (Carew) to intercept them if he could handsomely doe it". Carew readily undertook the job. He got the messenger waylaid and robbed; he took the letters at once to the Deputy, and when both had read them, returned to diue with his guest Don Juan! When the messenger, who had been robbed, arrived and told his tale, the Don complained bitterly to the Lord Deputy, but that worthy personage "seemed no less sorry; but (said he) it is a common thing in all armies to haue debaucht souldiers, but hee thought it to bee rather done by some of the country thieues; but if the fact was committed by souldiers, it was most like to bee done by some Irish men". The Don however strongly suspected Carew, and said so, but

the Deputy declared him innocent. In the end the pair
of rogues offered a large reward for the discovery of the
robber! The means employed by Carew for the capture
of the Earl of Desmond were in perfect keeping with the
foregoing. And on such transactions as these Sir George
prided himself very highly.

Note 9, Page 40.

" I have lost
Ancestral lands and castles fair".

The MacGeoghegans had high rank and large possessions in the County of Meath, all which they lost in
the long succession of wars which desolated that part
of the country.

Note 10, Page 46.

"Owen MacEggan, blest of God,
And faithful friar Neale".

On the 6th of June, the day on which the English
army disembarked on the mainland, the defenders of
Dunboy received intelligence that on the previous night
a Spanish ship with succours for them had arrived at
Ardea, in the bay of Kenmare. " Some Irish passengers
was in her (says the *Pacata*), namely, a fryar Iames
Nelane, a Thomond man belonging to Sir Tirlogh O'Brien,
who had charge of the treasure; Owen MacEggan, the
Pope's Bishop of Rosse, and his *Vicarius Apostolicus*,
with letters to sundry rebels, and twelve thousand
pounds. . . The distribution of the money by appoint-
ment in Spaine was left principally to the disposition
of Donnell O'Sulevan Beare. Owen MacEggan, Iames
Archer, and some others". This same Bishop MacEggan
was subsequently killed near Bandon, fighting gallantly
with his sword in one hand and his beads in the other.
His remains were buried in the abbey of Timoleague.

Note 11, Page 53.

"One hundred men and forty-four
In those narrow halls, not a mortal more;
Four thousand foemen round them".

Carew says the army with which he set out from Cork

for Dunboy "was in list neere three thousand, but by pole not exceeding fifteene hundred". This force was however recruited on its march, in accordance with his (Carew's) directions to "draw all the forces in the province to a head against them" (O'Sullivan and his friends). Near Bantry the army was joined by the regiment of Sir Charles Wilmot, who had been prosecuting the war in Kerry. Wilmot's force was "one thousand and seven hundred foote in list, but by pole very weak". It is therefore probable that the besieging force amounted in round numbers to about 4,000, which is the number given by Mitchel in his life of Hugh O'Neill. The number of defenders within the castle is set down by the *Pacata Hibernia* as 143. Another account says 144, which does not greatly alter the proportion or disproportion between the forces.

Note 12, *page 55.*

"Their guns from yonder rounded strand,
Their battery from the mountain slope".

Two guns were placed on a point of land on the north side of that on which the castle stood; four guns were placed on a height to the west of the castle, and it was this latter battery that beat it into ruins. From the moment those guns were planted the fall of the castle was a matter of certainty. Most of the castles in Ireland, at that time, had been built to resist small arms only; when attacked with cannon, they were easily destroyed.

Note 13, *Page 61.*

"But I hope that my name
In our annals of fame
Will be set in a small piece of writing".

This was not an unusual wish amongst Irish warriors; and in the *Pacata Hibernia*, amongst other documents connected with the defenders of Dunboy, is given a letter written the night before his execution by one John Anias to the Baron of Lixnaw, in which is the following passage :—

"As ever I aspire to immortalize my name upon the

Earth, so I would request you, by virtue of that ardent affection I had toward you in my life, you would honour my death in making mention of my name in the register of your country".

This John Anias was one "who concieved himself to be a good Ingeniere", as also, it would appear, did " Iames Archer, Iesuit"; letters from both of whom, referring to the fortification of Dunboy, are given in the *Pacata*.

Note 14, Page 73.
" Ho, Marshall, bear him to the block!"

" Vpon the fall thereof the enemy sent out a messenger offering to surrender the place, if they might haue their liues and depart with their armes, and a pledge given for the assurance thereof. Neverthelesse they continued shooting all the while the messenger was coming betweene them and us, whose message being delivered, the Lord President turned him over to the Marshall, by whose direction hee was executed"—*Pac. Hib.*

The bloodthirsty ferocity of this Carew and his army was unrestrained by any feeling of honour or humanity. The messenger from the castle should have been sent back when his terms were rejected, but rarely could Carew have an enemy in his power and not kill him. This will appear to any one who reads even his own account of his proceedings.

Note 15, Page 77.
" Bold O'More was seen to labour", etc.

Mellaghlan Moore, who was one of three soldiers who leaped from off a vault of the castle and was immediately slain, was, says Carew, " the man that layed hands first upon the Earle of Ormond, and plucked him from his horse, when he was taken prisoner by Owhny Mac Roury".

Note 16, Page 81.
" Firm in my hand the trusty lance
Grasped for the holy League of France".

" A Fryer, borne in Yoghall, called Dominicke Collins, who had been brought up in the Warres of Fraunce, and there under the League had been a Commander of Horse in Britanny"—*Pac. Hib.*

Note 17, *Page* 93.

" Friends and foes at once shall I
Hurl in one blast tow'rds the sky".

" Then MacGeohagan, chiefe commander of the place, being mortally wounded with divers shott in his body, the rest made choise of one Thomas Taylor, an English mans Sonne (the dearest and inwardest man with Tirrell, and married to his Neece), to be their chiefe, who having nine barrels of powder, drew himselfe and it into the Vault, and there sate downe by it, with a light match in his hand, vowing and protesting to set it on fire, and blow up the Castle, himselfe, and all the rest, except they might haue promise of life"—*Pac. Hib.*

Note 18, *Page* 96.

" That ere within the Saxon's camp
The headsman's strokes continued long,
With a steady champ, like a measured tramp,
For the clansmen's bones were stout and strong".

" The same day fiftie-eight were executed in the Market-place, but the Fryar, Taylor, and one Tirlagh Roe MacSwiney, a follower unto Sir Tirlagh O'Brian, and twelue more of Tirrells chiefe men, the Lord President reserved aliue to trie whether he could draw them to doe some more acceptable service than their lives were worth. The whole number of the ward consisted of one hundred and fortie-three selected fighting men, being the best choice of all their Forces, of the which no one man escaped, but were either slaine, executed, or buried in the mines, and so obstinate and resolved a defence had not bin seene within this Kingdome"—*Pac. Hib.*

Tirrell endeavoured to negociate with Carew to spare the lives of his twelve men. "Answer was returned to him, and a stratagem propounded, in the effecting thereof he should obtain pardon and libertie for himself and his dependants". What piece of villainy this " stratagem" was, Carew does not inform us ; but " the reply which he made thereunto was, that he would ransome the Prisoners with money, if that might be accepted ; but to be false to the King of Spaine (whom hee termed his master), or to betray the Catholicke cause, hee would never ; upon which answer his twelve men (before respited) two dayes after were executed". Taylor was carried on to Cork,

where he was hanged in chains, and Father Collins, who
would not "endeavour to merite his life by discovering
the Rebel's intentions (which was in his power), or by
doing of some service that might deserve favour, was
hanged at Youghall, the Towne where he was borne".

Note —*. page 99.

"Brothers their brothers' blood betray,
And clan on clan works ruin, while
The common foe wins all the Isle".

A glance into the history of those times will but too
fully bear out the statement in the lines above quoted.
In any country circumstances similar to those in which
Ireland was then placed would produce like results. But,
however this may be, the English policy of "divide and
conquer" worked its way amongst the O'Sullivans as
well as amongst other native families.

When Donal took up arms for his religion and country,
Owen, son to Sir Owen (mentioned in note 4), was led to
think that by remaining attached to the English govern-
ment, and by aiding the expedition of Carew against
Dunboy, he would get the partition which had been
made in his father's time quashed, and the land of Beare
granted to him. More than twelve months before the
English army proceeded to the siege of Dunboy, the Lord
President of Munster, Sir George Carew, despatched the
Earl of Thomond with a force of " 2,500 foote in list, to
make tryall whether the rebels in the countrey of Carbery
would submit themselves upon the sight of an army".
Amongst the instructions given to the Earl on this occa-
sion were the following :—

" The service you are to performe is to do all your
endeavour to burne the rebels Corne in Carbery, Beare,
and Bantry, take their cowes, and to use all hostile pro-
secution upon the persons of the people, as in such cases
of rebellion is accustomed.

" When you are in Beare (if you may without any apparent perill) your lordship shall doe well to take a view
of the castle of Dunboy, whereby wee may be the better
instructed how to proceed for the taking of it, when time
convenient shall be afforded.

---

* By a mistake, no reference figure was put to those lines in the
text.

"Giue all the comfort you may to Owen O'Sulevan, by whose means you know the affaires of those parts will best be composed".

Thomond proceeded to Bantry as directed, burned the rebels' corn in famous fashion, gave much wordy comfort to Owen O'Sullivan, but decided that there was " apparent perill" in attempting to get near Dunboy, inasmuch as Donal with a strong force stood in his way at Glengariffe. He contented himself with strengthening the garrison of Captain Flower at Bantry, and placing another garrison on Whiddy Island; he then returned to Carew with his report of the state of " affairs in those parts". Very soon after his departure Donal expelled his garrison from Whiddy Island. Owen O'Sullivan assisted in the reduction of Donal's forts on the Dursey Island, which was accomplished during the early days of the siege of Dunboy. It is no wonder he was a willing leader in that expedition, as his wife was then, and had for three months previously been, a prisoner in one of the forts. The *Pacata* does not say that Owen assisted at the siege of Dunboy itself. He captured, however, for the English the castle of Dunmanus, " and tooke the prey and spoyle of the towne". The writer has not learned what was his reward in the end. Most probably it was to have " prey and spoyle" taken from himself, to fail of getting his cousin Donal's possessions, and to lose his own.

Note 19, Page 100.

"And many a stately keep and dun
Back from their Irish allies won".

" The fall of Dunboy did not prevent the Prince of Beare from still acting a brave and noble part. Dermod O'Driscoll being returned from Spain, Cornelius, son of O'Driscoll More, was sent to solicit speedy assistance; in the meantime the Prince and Captain Tirrell marched with a thousand men into Muskerry, and made themselves masters of Carriag-na-Chori, Duin Dearaire, and Mocrumpe, where they placed a garrison, after which he prevailed upon O'Donoghue of the Glinne to join the confederacy; he made incursions into the districts of

Cork, and returned loaded with booty".—*MacGeoghe-gan's History of Ireland,* vol. III. cap. xiv.

Note 20, Page 101.

" Troops unkept by foreign aid,
Would famish in the wasted land".

The desolation of Munster, and of other parts of Ireland, at this time was frightful. Holinshed, Spenser, Davies, and others, give terrible pictures of it. The former says, " The whole country having no cattle nor kine left, they (the Irish) were driven to such extremities that, for want of victuals, they were either to die and perish by famine, or to die under the sword". And again, having spoken of the great numbers slain, he says : " After this followed an extreme famine, and such whom the sword did not destroy, the same did consume and eat out, for they were not only driven to eat horses, dogs, and dead carrions, but they also did devour the carcasses of dead men. . . . The land itself, which before these wars was populous, well-inhabited, and rich in all the good blessings of God, . . . is now become waste and barren, yielding no fruits, the pastures no cattle, the air no birds . . . Whosoever did travel from the one end to the other of all Munster . . he would not meet with any man, woman, or child, saving in towns and cities, nor yet see any beast, but the very wolves, the foxes, and other ravening beasts, and many of them lay dead, being famished, and the residue gone elsewhere". Spenser says : " Out of every corner of the woods and glynns they (the Irish) came creeping forth upon their hands, for their legs could not bear them ; they looked like anatomies of death ; they spake like ghosts crying out of their graves ; they did eat the dead carrions, happy when they could find them—yea, and one another soon after, insomuch as the very carcasses they spared not to scrape out of their graves, and if they found a plot of watercresses or shamrocks, there they flocked as to a feast for the time, ye not long able to continue there withal, that in a short space there were none almost left, and a most populous and plentiful country suddenly left void of man and beast".

Note 21, Page 102.

"He robbed the eaglets of their food
To feed the young O'Sullivans".

This is a well-preserved tradition in Beare and Bantry.

Note 22, Page 105.

"They fought by day, they fought at night".

In giving an account of the flight of O'Sullivan into Ulster, the Four Masters say : " He was not a day or night during that space without encountering desperate conflicts and severe pursuits, which were valiantly and promptly resisted by him". A detailed account of the flight is given in the annals, and in the *Historiæ Catholicæ Ibernicæ Compendium* of Don Philip O'Sullivan Beare. The Abbé MacGeoghegan, in his History of Ireland, says: " We read nothing more like to the expedition of Young Cyrus and the Ten Thousand Greeks, than this retreat of O'Sullivan Beare".

Note 23, Page 108.

" Turned from the bloody field, and fled".

" Neverthelesse, when they saw that they must make their way by the sword or perish, they gave a braue charge upon our men, in the which Captain Malby was slaine, upon whose fall Sir Thomas and his troops, fainting, with the losse of many men, studied their safeties by flight, and the rebels, with little harme, marched into Orwyke countrey"—*Pac. Hib.*

" O'Sullivan made an onset, with rage and anger, with fury and vehemence, towards the place where the English were, for against them was excited his entire vengeance and animosity, and he did not stop until he gained the place where he beheld their commander, and he fiercely and quickly cut off the head of the noble Englishman, namely, the son of Captain Malby; that collected force was afterwards defeated, and a great number of them were slain, and it is doubtful if the like number of a force, fatigued after a long march, and encompassed by their enemies as they were, performed such an exploit as they achieved that day in defence of their lives and renown"—*Annals of the Four Masters.*

11

Note 24, Page 110.

"In Spain, high placed beside the king".

" O'Neill, O'Donnell, O'Sullivan Beare, and some other Irish chiefs went the next summer to England to make their submission to James I , who had just succeeded Elizabeth, and to compliment him upon his accession to the throne of England. O'Sullivan being unable to obtain his pardon, sailed for Spain, and was well received by King Philip III., who created him knight of the military order of St. Iago, and afterwards Earl of Berehaven"—*MacGeoghegan's History.*

O'Sullivan received from the King of Spain a pension of 300 pieces of gold monthly. The manner of his death is thus told by his cousin Philip, in his Catholic History :—

" But the last stroke of adverse fortune befell thus :—On the eighteenth day of the same month (July, 1608), O'Sullivan, Prince of Beare, in whom all the hopes of)the Irish at that time were placed, unhappily perished in this manner. John Bath, an Anglo-Irishman, and one whom O'Sullivan held in very high esteem—even to the extent of taking him under his personal protection, bestowing many favours upon him, and even admitting him to his own table in the circle of his most intimate friends—quite ungrateful for such high favours, carried his presumption so far as that when a discussion arose touching some money advanced by O'Sullivan as a loan, he, Bath, dared to make unfavourable comparisons between a family, one of the most illustrious among the Irish, and the English, from whom he himself was sprung. Philip, the writer of this history, a cousin of O'Sullivan (*Philippus, O'Sullivani patruelis*), unable to endure this insult, expostulated with Bath upon the matter. The dispute proceeded so far that they attacked each other with drawn swords, at a royal monastery, not far from Madrid. In this contest, Bath, terror-stricken, kept retreating, shouting at the same time. Philip wounded him in the face, and, as it appears, would have slain him, had not Edmund O'Moore and Gerald McMorris (sent by O'Sullivan), and two Spanish knights, protected him, and Philip would have been himself arrested by a constable, but for their interference. When many were attracted to the spot by the quarrel, among others came O'Sullivan, a rosary in his left hand. Whilst thus incautious, fearing nothing, and looking in quite another direction, Bath approached him through the crowd, struck him through the left shoulder, and again piercing him through the throat, killed him. Philip hid himself in the house of the French ambassador, Marquis Seneccia from the constable, who vainly sought hi n. Bath was cast into prison, together with a relation of his, Francis Bath, who chanced to be present at the struggle. A relation to Philip, called O'Driscoll, was also imprisoned. O'Sullivan's interment, on the next day, was attended by a large concourse of Spanish nobles. He was fifty-seven years old at his death. He was an extremely pious, and a benevolent man to poor and needy, He was accustomed to hear two or three masses each day, and to spend a considerable time in prayer to God. He was tall and well built, with pleasing features".

In our modern Irish literature, Philip O'Sullivan, author of the Catholic History, has often been described as the son of Donal, the hero of Dunboy. Such description is incorrect. The father of Philip was Dermot O'Sullivan (a first cousin of Donal). The fact is repeatedly stated by Philip in his work, and a full account of his family is given by him in one of his poems, which is prefixed to the Dublin edition of the Catholic History.

THE END.

J. F. Fowler, Printer, 3 Crow Street, Dame Street, Dublin.